WAR ON THE PLAINS

The line of mounted warriors broke and poured forward, lances and war clubs waving overhead. Ramon Cabeza wheeled his horse and ran, hearing the thunder behind him, watching his pitiful platoon attempt to form a defensive position as he approached.

He yanked the gray stallion to a sliding stop and pivoted to face the oncoming rush. With the precision of trained professionals, the Spanish lancers swung into their short defensive charge. The two forces clashed, horses and men went down in the melee. The tangle swept toward the creek and the crossbowmen began to make themselves felt. Short, heavy crossbow bolts twanged, taking a deadly toll.

Cabeza slashed, parried, thrust and circled. He saw a lancer struck down, but another vaulted to the saddle to bring his lance into play. A young warrior loomed before him, swinging his stone club. Cabeza readied his sword.

It could not last much longer. More warriors were pounding across the meadow, anxious to count honors before the last Spaniard fell. The yipping falsetto war cry blended into a continuous high-pitched roar. . . .

Bantam Books by Don Coldsmith
Ask your bookseller for the books you have missed

The Spanish Bit Saga Book 1—TRAIL OF THE SPANISH BIT
The Spanish Bit Saga Book 2—THE ELK-DOG HERITAGE
The Spanish Bit Saga Book 3—FOLLOW THE WIND
The Spanish Bit Saga Book 4—BUFFALO MEDICINE
The Spanish Bit Saga Book 5—MAN OF THE SHADOWS
The Spanish Bit Saga Book 6—DAUGHTER OF THE EAGLE
The Spanish Bit Saga Book 7—MOON OF THUNDER
The Spanish Bit Saga Book 8—THE SACRED HILLS
The Spanish Bit Saga Book 9—PALE STAR
The Spanish Bit Saga Book 10—RIVER OF SWANS
The Spanish Bit Saga Book 11—RETURN TO THE RIVER
The Spanish Bit Saga Book 12—THE MEDICINE KNIFE
The Spanish Bit Saga Book 13—THE FLOWER IN THE
                                                            MOUNTAINS
The Spanish Bit Saga Book 14—TRAIL FROM TAOS
The Spanish Bit Super Editions—THE CHANGING WIND
                                                       THE TRAVELER
Rivers West, Volume 2: THE SMOKY HILL

Follow
the Wind

>> >> >> >> >> >> >> >> >> >> >> >> >>

DON COLDSMITH

BANTAM BOOKS
NEW YORK · TORONTO · LONDON · SYDNEY · AUCKLAND

RL 6, IL age 12 and up

This edition contains the complete text
of the original hardcover edition.
NOT ONE WORD HAS BEEN OMITTED.

FOLLOW THE WIND
A Bantam Domain Book / published by arrangement with
Doubleday & Company

PRINTING HISTORY
Doubleday edition published February 1983
Bantam edition / November 1987

DOMAIN and the portrayal of a boxed "d" are trademarks of Bantam Books,
a division of Bantam Doubleday Dell Publishing Group, Inc.

ISBN 0-553-26806-6

Published simultaneously in the United States and Canada

Bantam Books are published by Bantam Books, a division of Bantam
Doubleday Dell Publishing Group, Inc. Its trademark, consisting of the
words "Bantam Books" and the portrayal of a rooster, is Registered in
U.S. Patent and Trademark Office and in other countries. Marca Registrada.
Bantam Books, 666 Fifth Avenue, New York, New York 10103.

PRINTED IN THE UNITED STATES OF AMERICA

RAD   16   15   14   13   12   11   10   9   8

Introduction
by David Dary

For many people the Spanish heritage of the early
American West is often minimized in the hustle and
bustle of our modern world. In an age of super high-
ways, jet planes, space travel, communication satel-
lites, and countless other technological advancements,
the contributions of the early Spaniards seem rather
insignificant. Yet the Spanish were the first Europeans
to explore much of the American West. Between 1538
and 1542 Hernando de Soto want as far west as modern Oklahoma; Fray Marcos de Niza discovered the
Indian pueblos in the Southwest; and Francisco Vasquez
de Coronado traveled as far north as modern Kansas in
search of the Seven Cities of Cibola with their streets
paved in gold

Coronado and his expedition of thirty mounted men,
six foot soldiers and a Franciscan father, never found
the gold, but they did find a tribe of tall friendly
Indians, some more than six and a half feet in height.
The dark-skinned, tattooed, nearly naked Indians lived
in round, grass-covered houses and raised crops of

corn, beans, and melons. Coronado and his party were
the first Europeans to see these Indians, probably Wich-
itas, somewhere in what is now central Kansas.

Coronado and his party were pleased with the beauty
of the land, especially the gentle contour of the rolling
carpet of grass that stretched from horizon to horizon.
It was soft and inviting. Coronado's lieutenant Juan
Jaramillo described the soil as "rich and black," and
he noted that it was "well watered by arroyos, springs,
and rivers." He added: "It is not a hilly country, but
has tablelands, plains, and charming rivers with fine
waters. . . . I am of the belief that it will be very
productive of all sorts of commodities." For some members of Coronado's party, the land reminded them of
their native Spain.

They found wild plums, grapes, mulberries, nuts, and
countless bison grazing on the lush grasses. Jaramillo
observed that the buffalo were the Indian's principal
source of food, and the shaggy creatures roamed the
region in numbers "as large as anyone could imagine." The buffalo were the Indian's cattle.

The Spaniards, of course, were the first to bring
domestic cattle to the western hemisphere. Columbus
took them to the West Indies on his second voyage in
1494, less than fifty years before Coronado reached
modern Kansas. Cattle were soon taken to what is
now Mexico, and it was there that the cattle increased
in number. The Spaniards soon tired of caring for
them. Trusted Indians, *mestizos* (of mixed Spanish
and Indian parentage), and mulattoes (of mixed black
and white percentage) were given the job to look after
the cattle. The vaquero was born.

In time the vaquero was given the horse to do his
job better. Spanish cattle ranching soon spread northward through what is now Mexico and into modern
Texas and California. As the decades passed, the tools
and techniques of the mounted Spanish vaquero were
adopted and modified by the early Texians and Cali-
fornianos and the American cowboy was born. But
this was more than two centuries after Coronado and

his expedition rode their horses north from New Spain in search of gold.

Mounted on their horses, Coronado and his men were undoubtedly a strange sight for the Indians to behold. It probably was the first time the Indians had seen horses. Certainly the animal gave the Spaniards an advantage over the Indians, who were on foot. The animal provided speed and mobility. It was an advantage that was to last until the Indians eventually acquired the horse.

Although wild horses were indigenous to North America, for some unknown reason the animal disappeared about fifteen thousand years ago. It was the Spanish who brought the horse back to the western hemisphere late in the fifteenth century. Hernán Cortés took them to what is now Mexico in 1519, and other Spanish explorers, including De Soto and Coronado, rode horses on their expeditions. But none of the horses from these early Spanish expeditions apparently survived to produce progeny. There is a colorful tradition that strays from De Soto's expedition met strays from Coronado's somewhere in Texas, but if there is any truth to the legend, it has been lost in time.

It is known that after Spanish ranchers developed the open range system of pasturing cattle and horses, some horses on ranches along the Rio Grande in present-day New Mexico were taken by dissatisfied Pueblo Indians working as servants for the Spaniards. Some of these Indians joined up with buffalo-hunting Indians on the southern plains. With the tame and well-broken horses stolen from the Spanish, these Pueblo Indians soon taught the Plains Indians how to care for the horses, and they passed along their skill in breaking, handling, and using horses. As time passed, these Indians gave or traded horses to other tribes and passed along the knowledge of how to use and care for the animals. Between 1650 and 1770 all Indian tribes in the West acquired horses, including descendants of the Indians who met Coronado more than a century earlier in present-day Kansas.

The horse had a profound influence on those Indians who depended upon the buffalo for food. With the horse, no longer did whole tribes—men, women, and children—have to go on buffalo hunts. Only the men mounted on horseback were required to hunt, and they could more easily kill buffalo for meat and robes. In turn the horse gave the Indians more leisure time, and it was used to develop the complex and colorful Plains Indian culture that flowered during the nineteenth century.

During the years following Coronado's 1541 expedition, other mounted Spaniards undoubtedly crisscrossed the plains, but few accounts exist to tell of their adventures. Most of their expeditions were not officially sanctioned by the Spanish crown. One unauthorized expedition of which there is a record was captained by Francisco de Leyva y Bonilla and Antonio Gutierrez de Humana. They left what is now New Mexico in 1593 or 1594 and traveled east and north into modern Kansas, searching for the legendary "gold mines of Tindan." But they found no gold, only death. One night near a large river—perhaps the Smokey Hill or Kansas—one of the Spaniards and five Indian servants deserted the expedition. Later on another night a few days later, Indians of the region set fire to grass on all sides of their camp, and the remaining Spaniards were burned alive.

Although there are few reminders on the Great Plains of the early Spanish explorers, the Spanish heritage is still visible in the architecture of many western homes, businesses, and churches. It is apparent in the countless place names of cities, towns, villages, creeks, rivers, canyons, and many other things. And it is heard in some of the words sprinkled through the modern American's daily speech, Spanish words corrupted over the years by their English pronunciation. For instance, the word ranch was derived from the Spanish word *rancho*, meaning "farm." And among modern American cowboys the word hackamore is a corruption of

FOLLOW THE WIND   >> ix

the Spanish word *jaquima* (hah-ke-mah), meaning
halter. The word *mecate*, meaning a horses's reins
made of horsehair rope, was also corrupted by American cowboys and called "McCarty"; and the word
lasso comes from the Spanish word *lazo*—a rope with
a slipknot.

The spanish heritage is also very evident in this
novel, *Follow the Wind*, by Don Coldsmith. He tells
about one such unauthorized Spanish expedition late
in the sixteenth century. In this third novel in a series, he captures the romance and significance of
the land, the wide-open spaces and vast distances that
had to be traversed, and he leaves no doubt about the
importance of the horses to the Spanish.

Coldsmith, a physician, is a native Kansan who
nearly three decades ago settled on the edge of the
Kansas Flint Hills, a modern cattle ranching region
which probably was crisscrossed by one or more early
Spanish explorers. The influence of this land and its
early recorded history spurred Coldsmith's interest in
researching and writing about the early Spanish, the
Indians, and the horse. While his characters and the
unauthorized Spanish expedition are fictional, the history is real. His descriptions of the land and the times
are factual. While fictional in name only, his friendly
Indian tribe—the People—is actually a composite of
four real tribes—Kiowa, Comanche, Cheyenne, and
Arapahoe—that inhabited the southern plains. The
way of life of the People is essentially that of the real
tribes of the reigon and period.

Coldsmith's story is delightful reading. He captures
the flavor and spirit of a time when the Spanish
were more active in the American West than most
Americans realize. He reminds us of the role played
by the Spanish in the history of the early American
West, and of a heritage that should not be forgotten.

Along the Kaw
Lawrence, Kansas
April, 1987

1

>> >> >>

Sanchez leaned his elbows on the rough planks of the table and sipped his wine. It was poor wine, but inexpensive. In his fuzzy half-drunken stupor, it didn't matter much anyway. One wine tasted much like another after so many hours of carousing. So he drank the cheap red house wine and wondered dreamily where his next meal was coming from.

He glanced around the tavern and decided that none of the clientele was worth his time. After all, the risk of being caught picking a pocket was hardly worth the few centavos, perhaps a peso or two. And surely, none of these patrons appeared affluent enough to have more than that. A very inferior quality of customers, he thought haughtily.

The sound of horses in the street roused Sanchez from reverie and he shuffled toward the door to look. He was careful to take his tankard with him. One could never trust anyone, he mused. Someone might drink his wine. At the thought, he glanced quickly around the room, but everyone had picked up his own wine, probably for the same reason.

Distrustful pigs, thought Sanchez. Unable to better his situation by purloining anyone's drink, he moved on toward the doorway, shoving between two other patrons to see better.

The procession was grand to behold. He blinked for a moment in the bright sunlight. As his eyes became accustomed to the sudden brilliance of the afternoon, he saw an elderly man, dressed in the finest of clothing, astride a magnificent gray horse. Uniformed men-at-arms flanked him on either side and a coach, pulled by four black horses, followed behind. Sanchez could catch a glimpse of a woman's profile behind the lacy curtains of the fancy carriage. A liveried footman sat beside the uniformed driver on the high seat.

Bringing up the rear were three more men-at-arms, well dressed, well equipped. The entire impression was that of wealth.

Ah, thought Sanchez, the rich know how to live! Curious, he shuffled back to the table and motioned to the tavern keeper, who came forward with ready jug. Sanchez shook his head and covered his tankard with cupped palm. He had no more money and wished to conceal from the host that he was nursing the last finger of wine very slowly so he could sit longer in the cool shade.

"Who is the old man in the street?"

"Ah, señor, you are truly a stranger to this town! That is Don Pedro Garcia and the señora, Doña Isabel."

Sanchez nodded and sipped his wine. The name nudged faintly at his memory. No, probably someone he had never heard of. There were many Garcias. He had asked only from idle curiosity. He was fascinated by those of wealth, largely because they had wealth, making them more profitable to steal from.

The tavern keeper was rattling on, the gossipy conversation of a local, telling an outsider about his town.

"—and it nearly killed the old man when his only son was lost in New Spain."

Suddenly, Sanchez became alert. Mother of God, could

it be? That young officer, lost and presumed dead on the plains. His name had been Garcia, had it not?

"What was the son's name?" He tried to appear casual.

"Let me see," the tavern keeper mused. He remembered the young man, who had been a hard drinker, something of a rascal, in an exuberant, youthful sort of way. "Juan, I think it was. Yes, that's right. Juan Garcia. Their only child, you see." He shook his head sympathetically.

"And what happened to him?" Sanchez was certain now, but remained covert in his conversation. What a stroke of good fortune!

"Why, he was lost on an expedition to the north of New Spain. Killed by savages, I suppose. It was about five years ago. They found no gold either, I'm told."

Yes, too bad, thought Sanchez. He had counted on a share of that gold when he enlisted. But there had been no gold. Only mile after mile of the endless grassland.

And young Garcia. Sanchez remembered well the day he had struck off by himself with a lance. He was never seen again. The next day, the Capitan had turned back. The men had discussed Garcia's probable fate around the campfires on the return journey. Most believed that he had been killed by savages or that he had wandered until he starved. He could have been captured, of course. There had been that one other soldier he had heard of. What was his name? No matter. The story was that he had been found six years later, living with the savages.

And it was just this sort of unresolved doubt that began to incubate the seed of a scheme in the evil little mind of Sanchez. He could pretend to have information of the only son of Don Pedro Garcia. The old man might pay handsomely for the story. What matter that it was untrue? And who was to say that it was? The leader of the expedition, Sanchez had heard, was in disfavor with the authorities. Many of the group were dead now. By the time Don Pedro learned anything to the contrary, Sanchez would be long gone with whatever gold the old man had been willing to give.

He finished his wine at one gulp. This completely confused the tavern keeper, who had seen Sanchez nurse the same thimbleful for half the afternoon. Casually, the guest asked directions to the hacienda of Don Pedro Garcia and departed into the fading afternoon sun.

Sanchez was beginning to devise a tale of magnificent proportions. He would wait until full dark before his approach. Any tale is better for the telling by candlelight.

2
>> >> >>

The guard at the heavy iron gate agreed to send word of the visitor to the *Señor* Garcia and, in due course, a house servant came back with the message. Don Pedro knew no Sanchez and refused to see him. Sanchez was rebuffed for only a moment.

"Tell him," he shouted after the retreating servant, "that I have news of his son!"

Within a short while, Sanchez was escorted into the big house and was seated across a small table from Don Pedro. The old man called for wine and poured a glass for each of them, candlelight sparkling in the clear red fluid.

Sanchez sipped, savoring the moment. This fault-lessly dressed and groomed old man, silver hair and beard shining, would have to wait until he, Sanchez, was ready. The guest settled back on his chair, sipping again from his glass. Let the rich bastard wait. Why, that heavy gold ring on his middle finger, with the big jewel in it, would keep Sanchez eating well for a month. He wondered if he should mention a specific amount for his reward.

Don Pedro sat and watched the scruffy little man opposite him. Sanchez sipped, tiny droplets of the excellent wine clinging to the hairs of his sparse moustache.

Finally, the old man cleared his throat gently.

"You said you have word of my son? How can this be?" He appeared hardly able to restrain his eagerness.

"Ah yes, *patron*," the other nodded. "Your son— Juan, I believe, is his name?" He was careful to avoid use of the past tense. The old man would be worth a bigger reward if he thought his son still alive.

Don Pedro nodded, still distrustful. Anyone might know the name. "Yes, go on."

"I was with the expedition."

The old man became more interested.

"How do I know that?"

Sanchez spread his hands in bewilderment. He had not foreseen this shrewd questioning. He must think fast.

"The young officer Garcia rode a gray mare."

Correct, but still meaningless. Don Pedro shrugged. The Garcia horses were widely known and many were grays.

"The mare was called Lolita, *señor*."

How fortunate that he had happened to remember that fact, Sanchez thought. He saw that the old man was now convinced. Now he could savor the scene, playing with the older man like a cat with a mouse. Let the bastard suffer a bit. Then maybe he'll pay more. He leaned back, sipped the good wine, and waited.

The patience of Don Pedro Garcia appeared to be wearing thin.

"Yes, go on." More firmly now.

Sanchez spread his palms in an exaggerated shrug.

"*Señor* Garcia, I had thought that there might be some mention of a reward for the less fortunate person who could bring you such information."

His tone was fawning and ingratiating, his smile oily.

In the next few heartbeats, Sanchez became very suddenly aware that he had not only overplayed his hand, but badly underestimated his man. He found himself flat on his back, his overturned chair under him. In the center of his chest was a bony knee. The point of a dagger pressed gently against the soft part of Sanchez's throat between the jawbones in a most businesslike manner. His head was immobilized by a firm grip on a handful of his greasy hair. The old don was surprisingly strong and agile.

"Son of a mangy dog," Garcia hissed between clenched teeth. "Your reward will be that you will be allowed to live a little longer. But only if you talk rapidly enough!"

Sanchez swallowed hard, the very motion bringing the needle-sharp point of the knife more firmly against his skin. He tried hard to assume a facial expression of complete cooperation. Apparently he was successful, for the firm grip of the other began to relax a little.

"Your pardon, señor," the sweating Sanchez whined. "I meant no harm. Surely, to serve one so noble as yourself is all the reward one could wish for."

Don Garcia said nothing, but released his prisoner and sheathed the knife. He waited expectantly, not in any way believing the fawning apology. Sanchez was thinking rapidly. He must be convincing now. He had very nearly destroyed the entire effort in trying to be too clever. He cleared his throat to continue.

"I have reason to believe your son is alive."

The old don reached casually for his weapon again and Sanchez hurried on.

"No no, señor, I speak truth! You must know that his body was never found."

This much, at any rate, was true. It had been stated, with regrets, in a letter from the Capitan. But what else?

Sanchez, meanwhile, was rapidly fabricating a new story, modifying it as he went. He would use the facts of that other case—what in Christ's name had been the details? No matter—it had happened on the Gulf Coast—a Spanish prisoner of the savages. He had been found six years later to be living happily with them, with a native wife and children. Now, if Sanchez could remember enough of the details to transport the story north to the grassy prairie.

"I have heard," he continued, "from a friend who was with an expedition last year. They heard of a young man, a Spaniard, living with one of the bands of savages."

Anxiously, he peered at the silver-bearded face. Would the old man accept this fabrication, which was the wildest of sheer fantasy?

"Nonsense!" snorted Garcia. "There was no expedition to the north of New Spain last year."

Still, the tone of his voice said that he wanted to be convinced. Sanchez, with the cunning of long practice, knew that he was reading his quarry correctly now.

"Ah yes, *but*," his tone became confidential, "surely the *señor* is aware, there are those who cross the river while the authorities look the other way."

Yes, nodded Don Pedro. He knew there were illegal expeditions, mostly looking for gold. He had heard of at least one colony mining with native slave labor without the proper legal authorization. All those things lent credence to the other's tale.

"Of course, it may not be your lost son," Sanchez shrugged helplessly, "even though it was in the same area where he was separated from us."

That was the final nudge, he saw. He drained his glass and rose to approach the door, waiting for the other's call.

"Wait!" came the crisp command. Sanchez turned expectantly. Now the old man, remorseful over his previous treatment, would give him gold and he would depart.

"Sit down," came the invitation, now more a request than a command.

"Could you," continued the old patriarch, "take me with an expedition to the area where you last saw him?"

Sanchez was hard put to conceal his astonishment.

He had expected the old man to apologetically offer a few pesos and that would be the end of it.

Now, this put a whole new light on the matter. The quick mind of the scoundrel immediately accepted the rapidly changing situation. Never had he had quite such a glorious opportunity. Delusions of grandeur filled his head.

In his imagination, he saw himself in fine clothes, riding one of the beautiful Garcia horses. He pointed ahead and the entire column moved forward, sunlight gleaming on polished armor.

Don Pedro Garcia cleared his throat, bringing the dreamer back to reality.

"Of course, *Señor* Garcia," he nodded eagerly.

What matter that there was nothing there to look for or that he, Sanchez, had no idea of the route? He would be able to convince the old man that he knew where he was going.

Most importantly, he would for many months be in contact with those of great wealth. There would be innumerable opportunities to steal. Perhaps, even, to exact a little vengeance for that embarrassing scene with the dagger. But all that could come later. For now, the saints had smiled on Sanchez this day.

"I would be honored to be allowed to serve you," he purred.

3

>> >> >>

There was much grumbling in the kitchens and stables of the Garcia estate. The newcomer was viewed with suspicion at first, then distrust, and finally scorn and ridicule. The servants quickly recognized Sanchez for the scoundrel that he was. There was much wonder that such a charlatan could so completely sway the usually keen judgment of Don Pedro.

For his part, Sanchez did little to endear himself to the household staff. He was swaggering, demanding, and insolent, strutting in his new finery and assuming the affected mannerisms that he believed belonged to the rich. He was aware that the lowliest of the Garcia servants laughed behind his back and this only made him more arrogant and disagreeable.

He was especially piqued at Don Pedro's attitude. The old man firmly demanded that the household maintain an appearance of respect for the guest. Just as firmly, however, he refused to give Sanchez free rein where money was concerned. He doled out small

10

amounts to the infuriated scoundrel, whose hatred grew daily. Still, Sanchez was determined to swallow his pride in the hope of something bigger.

The two clashed repeatedly over the planning and equipage of the expedition. Sanchez had grandiose ideas as to the size, type, and expenditures appropriate for the venture. He had suggested a battery of at least two small cannons. Don Pedro had no particular aversion to cannons, though he considered them unnecessary. His main objection was that transportation over long distances would be slow and difficult. To his experienced mind, it seemed that cannons would merely impede the progress of the expedition. He well remembered fighting forces in the campaigns in southern France, encumbered by artillery mired in the mud. In the end, he refused to consider such equipment.

Similarly, Sanchez had envisioned a prestigious, heavily armed force of foot soldiers. They would need, he insisted, a platoon of arquebusiers. Here Don Pedro flatly refused to even consider such a thing. The old soldier had no use for such newfangled nonsense. There was something of black magic about the sulfurous-smelling troops with their smoldering matches. Besides, the entire scheme seemed somehow heretical to the old don. He could not have explained why he felt no objection to the burning of gunpowder in a cannon, but felt the same principle almost immoral in a small shoulder arm. A man should, by Christ, be able to fight like a man, not stand back at a safe distance and throw tiny projectiles at his enemies. He flatly forbade such a thing for this expedition.

As a compromise, however, Don Pedro did agree to a squad of crossbowmen. He had seen such units deployed with deadly efficiency against poorly organized foot troops. In addition, a single skilled marksman could use the accurate weapon to incapacitate the enemy by striking down their leaders. The old don suspected that even this was not quite a legitimate and manly device, but it was occasionally practical and useful. And above all, Don Pedro was a practical man.

The main force of men-at-arms would be mounted lancers. Mobile and effective, the platoon of lancers would give the impression of strength as well as offering real protection to the expedition. They would be uniformed, well trained, and mounted on the finest of the great Garcia Andalusians.

Don Pedro had already selected his lieutenant to command the lancers. He was Ramon Cabéza, son of an old comrade. The young man had distinguished himself at the Academy and showed much promise as a leader.

To round out the company, there were a number of foot servants. While all the Garcia servants had some training in the use of weapons, their major function would be as baggage carriers.

And there would be much baggage. Don Pedro had studied all the information he could find about New Spain when his son had departed for the area. He had since talked to a number of acquaintances who had taken part in such expeditions. It was not without some background of knowledge that he began plans for this journey.

Previous expeditions had not been able to deal effectively with the savages of the plains. Don Pedro would use an entirely different approach. Where others had relied on coercion, even torture, to gain information, Don Pedro proposed to buy it with gifts. He was not necessarily opposed to force as a method, but it had been demonstrated that with these natives it had been ineffective. Therefore, reasoned the old don, why not try the other method? In his experience, there was little that could not be achieved with either force or bribery. Many situations were eased by the greasing of a palm with silver.

With this in mind, the expedition would carry trade goods. Knives, mirrors, and ornaments of metal should be acceptable, he believed. In addition, there was a small chest with bags of coin—gold and silver to be used for expenses along the route.

Sanchez did little to conceal his contempt for the idea of trading goods as gifts in exchange for information. He would have spent the money involved for more military strength. Repeatedly, Don Pedro stubbornly planted his feet and refused to listen. At least twice, he found it necessary to call the attention of his unsavory guest to the fact that it was, after all, he, Don Pedro, who was the leader and financier of the expedition.

Once this occurred with servants present, embarrassing Sanchez before those he now considered beneath him. This added to his smoldering resentment and he dreamed of the day when he might exact vengeance. He had not decided what form it might take, but when the time came, he would know.

Meanwhile, as preparations continued, Ramon Cabeza selected and proceeded with the training of his lancers. Don Pedro was pleased with the young man's judgment, both in choice of men and of horses. His troop worked hard, becoming efficient quite rapidly. Cabeza, demonstrating that he was willing to work as hard as his men, earned immediate respect.

The young man viewed the entire project with mixed emotions. The prospect of a command in an expedition to New Spain was most enticing. It would be well financed, well equipped, and under the command of his father's old friend Don Pedro, long respected as a great warrior.

On the other hand, there was an element of doubt as to the purpose of the expedition. He had known Juan Garcia at the Academy, although they had not been close friends. He had been somewhat younger than Garcia. Now he, Ramon, was to be involved in a venture to search for the missing son of Don Pedro. Such a search in the vastness of the unexplored continent was surely a doubtful goal at best. And when there was added the element that the party's guide would be the insufferable Sanchez, the doubt tended to broaden.

After much soul-searching, Ramon finally mentioned his fears to the ancient Garcia family retainer who supervised the stables.

"Pablo, what do you think of this plan to search for the young Garcia?"

The old man looked keenly at his questioner for a long moment, then spread his hands in an exaggerated shrug.

"*Quién sabe!* Don Pedro has often been right."

There was one slight incident during these weeks of preparation, nipped in the bud by Cabeza. He happened to overhear a couple of his lancers in conversation in the stable after practice. One was chuckling at the futility of the expedition and the other responded with a partly heard remark about the "crazy old man."

Cabeza, furious, descended on the two like a whirlwind.

"Don Pedro," he hissed through clenched teeth, "was a great soldier when you still wet your beds at night!"

He dismissed them both, adding a comment for the benefit of a few who overheard.

"If you take a man's silver, you owe him allegiance, not ridicule!"

In the dark shadows of a stall, old Pablo smiled to himself. This young man would be a fitting lieutenant to serve Don Pedro.

4
>> >> >>

BILL OF LADING

One gray mare, 5 yrs., well reined (personal mount of
  Don Pedro Garcia).
One brown mare, 6 yrs., 4 white feet, white face.
Three gray mares, jennet-bred.
Eleven roan or gray stone-horses.
One black stone-horse, white left rear foot (property of
  Ramon Cabeza).
Don Pedro Garcia, patron.
Ramon Cabeza, Lt. of lancers.
Sixteen lancers, with arms.
H. Sanchez (who states that he is the guide).
Six crossbowmen, with arms.
Seven men.
Supplies of maize and hay for the crossing.
Six boxes of trade goods.
Two chests of personal effects of Sr. Garcia and party.

Don Pedro, Ramon, and Sanchez stood at dockside and watched as the cargo was lifted or hauled aboard the *Paloma*. The newly fitted galleon, with snowy white sails furled on her masts, appeared most satisfactory for the journey. The horses, along with their grain and hay, had been stowed in the spacious belly of the ship.

There had been a bit of trouble about the horses. The royal decree prohibiting export of horses was still in effect and Oliviera, the Portugee who commanded the vessel, became balky. Cabeza suggested that perhaps they might take only their personal mounts and buy more for the lancer platoon in Santo Domingo.

Ultimately, the prestige and the gold of Don Pedro Garcia paved the way and he was able to present a letter signed by local port authorities to the ship's master. The horses were quickly loaded.

Sailors scampered aloft and the *Paloma* spread her white wings to the sea breeze to begin the journey.

During the voyage, Don Pedro became fast friends with the ship's captain. He and the Portugee, an aging seaman and man of the world, recognized each other for contemporaries: Each could respect the other as a professional in a slightly different realm, related indirectly to his own.

There were long talks over the excellent wine carried in the cabin of Oliviera. Don Pedro, at length, confided the exact nature of his mission.

"Ah, my friend, I too had a son." The old seaman poured more wine and a tear glistened in his eye. "He was lost at sea off Hispaniola on his first voyage."

They drank to the memory of Oliviera's son and to the hope of finding Garcia's.

"Wait!" the host suddenly exclaimed. "I have something to show you!"

He stepped unsteadily across the cabin and unlocked a lacquered box. Carefully, he drew forth a rolled parchment and spread it on the table. Don Pedro's eyes lighted with interest. It was a map, one of great beauty and detail, executed in full color. Well-drawn sketches of caracels and galleons ornamented the oceans and a whale spouted in the southern sea.

Don Pedro knew something of maps from his long experience in the military and he recognized this as the latest in charts of the Americas. The Latin inscription modestly proclamed—A NEW WORLD, NEW DESCRIPTION.

"You see," Oliviera was pointing, "this is the new Mercator projection. The map is done by Ortelius. The straight lines are compass courses."

This was beyond the knowledge of Garcia, but he could see that the upper and lower portions of the map were elongated laterally. He was vaguely aware that global maps were a problem to sea navigation. A problem, representing a picture of something round on a flat surface. Oliviera was obviously impressed with this latest advance and extremely proud of his map. He warmed to the subject, but at last realized he was boring his guest.

"Ah, forgive me, my friend! This is of no matter. Here is what I wished to show you!" He poked a gnarled finger at a spot north of the area marked HISPANA NOVA. "There is where you are going!"

Don Pedro studied the chart for a long time. The ship rocked gently and a timber creaked. In the ship's belly, a horse stamped nervously.

"But, my friend," Garcia protested, "there is nothing there!"

"Exactly! Little is known of the area to the north."

Along the coast of the great gulf, as yet unnamed, from the projection labeled LA FLORIDA to that on the southwest called IUCATAN, there were charted the mouths of streams. These streams wandered inland in no particular fashion and stopped.

Suddenly, Garcia understood. The coast had been largely explored by ship. Landmarks were mostly those that could be seen from the sea. Further inland, very little had been charted. There was simply a large white space representing most of the continent, made even larger by the distortion of the new map's technique. Here and there were clusters of mountains, apparently placed at random by the artist, because nothing was known of the area. For the first time, Garcia realized with dread how fully he was dependent on the memory of the untrustworthy Sanchez.

"We will stop at Matanca on the north coast of Cuba," Oliviera was saying. "There we take on supplies and water. Then I will put in here," he pointed to an indentation on the coast of New Spain marked BAIA DE CULATA. "There is a good harbor and you can follow the river northward. I will return to this harbor for you a year from now."

So it was arranged. Garcia made a rough sketch of the area in question, knowing that it would be of practically no use once they left the coast.

The *Paloma* dropped anchor in the deep sheltered bay on the coast of New Spain. Horses were pushed over the side to swim ashore. Supplies and men were rowed ashore in the longboat and kegs of fresh water were returned from the river for use on the ship.

Camp was established near the beach, under the whispering palms, and the expedition bedded down for the first night in New Spain. Don Pedro walked alone to the edge of the darkness to gaze northward. He observed the constellation Ursa Major pointing to the Pole Star. Strange, how their appearance seemed the same here in strange foreign skies as in the land of his birth.

And what lay ahead in the vastness of the uncharted land? Would they be able to locate his son? Why, if Juan were still alive, had he not returned to his own people?

The old man listened to the unfamiliar voices of unknown creatures of the night in the dark canebrakes along the river. For the first time, he began to doubt the practicality of his mission. How could they find any trace of a missing individual in a continent so huge as that stretching before him in the starlight? Even the map makers had very little idea of the size or shape beyond the coastal areas.

Then there was Sanchez. Don Pedro knew the man could not be trusted. He had known from the first, but had grasped at the possibility that the little man might be able to guide him to the area where his son Juan had disappeared.

Perhaps he still could. After all, they had come this far. Maybe, just maybe, Sanchez would make good on his boast to guide the expedition. Something about the warm earthy smell of the river calmed the old man and created a feeling of optimism and confidence.

Don Pedro heaved a deep sigh and turned to his blankets. Why should the venture not be successful? He had fought against greater odds and won. The fact that he was alive today was proof.

5
» » »

Early next morning, the *Paloma* set sail with the tide. The party on the beach watched the galleon quarter around the headland and disappear. For a time, they could see the tip of her mainsail above the protective island reef that skirted along the shore and then she was gone. They were alone in the New World.

Sanchez viewed the morning with mixed feelings. He had, before the end of his previous expedition to New Spain, been utterly disillusioned. Now, at times, he could scarcely believe that he had voluntarily returned to this godforsaken continent. Only the possibility of financial gain could have made him do so.

Just now, such possibility seemed extremely remote. Instead, he was experiencing the reality that lay ahead. Heat, dust, thirst, hunger, and danger would be their lot. To add to all this was the gnawing doubt in Sanchez's scheming mind. Not as much doubt, actually, as a certainty. One that he dare not share with the others. The certainty was that he, Sanchez, had not the slightest idea where they were going. The previous expedition, of which he had been a part, had not come this way.

Oliviera had told them of a native village a half day's journey up the river. Beyond that, another two days, was an outpost, the last Spanish garrison on the frontier. They would spend the first night with the presumably friendly savages. At least, thought Sanchez, this first day or two would postpone the inevitable. Sooner or later would come the moment of truth. He would be forced to fabricate a reasonably believable story about the direction of the march.

Meanwhile, he would assume a knowing air and carry on the pretense. The others need not know that he had no clear idea where he was. And, after all, what did it matter? The young Garcia was probably long dead anyway. Sanchez could lead the expedition in a random fashion out onto the plains, pretending knowledge of the area. They would ask a few questions of any wandering tribes they might encounter. Then, when the weather or the terrain or the stamina of the old man began to become a problem, Sanchez could diplomatically convince the others that the mission was a failure.

It was primarily luck that led Sanchez to spot the snake. He was riding in the lead to help establish his position as guide. The trail was impossible to lose, skirting along the river, obviously well used, and plainly leading to the village they sought.

In a low area, the path swung somewhat away from the stream to avoid a thick growth of cane. There, directly in the trail, sprawled one of the thick-bodied serpents that Sanchez hated. The creature had sought out a level spot in which to sun. Speckles of shade from a scraggly tree nearby blended with the mottled skin of the snake and it became almost invisible to a casual observer. Thus, it was sheer good fortune that Sanchez happened to notice a subtle difference in the coloration of the object in the trail. He reined the mare sharply and cried a warning, just as the big rattler of the canebrake sounded his warning buzz.

"Look out! Mother of God!"

The palms of his hands were sweaty. In fact, his whole body seemed damp and clammy in his clothes. The sight of these wretched creatures always affected him this way. He had seen a man die from the poisonous bite. An agonizing death it was, with the affected limb bloating and bleeding internally, the shiny blood-filled blisters growing by the hour.

The mare snorted and fidgeted, nervous over something unfamiliar. Sanchez sat frozen in the saddle, barely able to maintain control of the frightened horse. Slowly, the great snake, as long as a man is tall, moved from the striking position and seemed to flow smoothly toward the shelter of the canebrake. Its motion was deliberate, almost slow, yet in the space of a few seconds the travelers were staring blankly at a mottled patch of shade which no longer held any living creature. The snake was gone.

Don Pedro, riding at Sanchez's stirrup, exhaled audibly and a murmur ran back along the column. It was their first encounter with one of the unknown hazards of the New World and all had heard tales of poisonous reptiles.

Sanchez sat for a moment, trying to regain his composure. He gulped deeply and took a deep breath. The mare instinctively moved ahead and the shaken rider allowed her to do so. Now that the incident was past, he began to worry again about appearances. Had he lost his composure too obviously? Anxiously, he glanced back down the line.

What he saw was only that the men behind him were concerned, too. Those on foot, especially, cast apprehensive looks at the dim recesses of the brake and skirted the growth by a wide margin.

Sanchez need not have worried. The net result of the encounter was to increase his prestige. It was, after all, he who had shouted the warning and stopped the column.

Slowly, he began to understand. There was respect in the way the men looked at him, in the way they spoke during the noon halt. It was very difficult for

him. No one, in all his life, had ever looked at him
with admiration and respect. Even those he had called
his friends had not shown these emotions. Theirs had
been merely a relationship of tolerance, with perhaps
less mutual distrust than they held for the rest of the
world. He would not have trusted them, nor would
they have trusted him, beyond the price of the next
glass of wine.

Sanchez began to enjoy the new experience. It was a
heady thing, a lift such as one felt from the rapid
consumption of good wine on an empty stomach. He
relaxed, chuckling inwardly in sheer enjoyment. So
this was how it felt to be respected! A resolve began
to form in the dark cobwebby recesses of his devious
little mind. As yet, it was beneath the level of his
consciousness, but it was there.

Certainly, there was no morality or conscience involved, no sense of right and wrong. The possibility
that respect was something to be earned had yet to
occur to him. At this point, Sanchez had discovered
only one fact. There was a better feeling when one
was admired than when one was hated and despised.

Yet another opportunity was to occur that day. They
reached the Caddo village of thatched dwellings and
little children ran to peer wonderingly from a safe
distance. A man approached, cautiously at first, and
led them to a larger structure which appeared to be a
council house or meeting place.

Sanchez found, rather to his surprise, that he remembered some of the sign language gestures the
native was using. Experimentally, he attempted the
sign for "leader" and that for "question."

"Your leader?"

The man nodded and motioned them into the meet-
inghouse. It took a few moments to adjust their eyes
to the dimness of the structure. There was no one to
be seen, but soon a group of natives entered and a
man, who appeared to be their chief, sat in a prominent position facing the visitors.

Communication was very difficult for a time, until
the native chief sent for a young man who could

speak some Spanish. He had, he told them haltingly, worked for the garrison two sleeps north.

Sanchez was in his glory. He squatted across from the young Caddo, made numerous meaningless gestures, and voiced monosyllables totally without significance. He had realized that the members of his own party, in their ignorance, would assume him to be conversing in the language of the savages. Meanwhile, the natives would believe the tirade of gibberish to be Spanish, which they did not understand. Sanchez would thus appear to be a masterful linguist and negotiator.

Despite all the playacting, some things were accomplished. The party would spend the night in the council house. Arrangements for food were made and gifts were given to the chief.

Almost as an afterthought, Sanchez negotiated for the services of the young Caddo with a slight knowledge of Spanish. He could be very useful in communicating with native tribes in the interior.

And, it must be confessed, Sanchez had also realized that to have someone to order around would increase his own prestige.

"Lizard," the young man came to be called. His name was an appellation so long and unpronounceable, full of clicks and guttural hisses, that the travelers gave up in despair.

The young guide had a rather heavy lower jaw, wide mouth and prominent cheekbones. Someone suggested that his face looked like that of a lizard and the name stuck. Neither he nor his temporary employers realized that, in fact, this was very close to a translation of his name in his own language. He had, in fact, for most of his life been called "The Lizard."

Sanchez had made certain, partially through his charade of meaningless gibberish, that Lizard understood that he must report only to him. This gave Sanchez more control over the situation. If their interpreter and guide had no one else to whom he could report, Sanchez could manipulate any situation to his own advantage.

They set out early the next morning, Sanchez riding in the lead, with Lizard trotting on foot alongside. Again, it would be next to impossible to miss the trail and these first days would establish the cunning Sanchez as leader of the column. Later, he thought vaguely, if the situation appeared to become dangerous, that arrogant young pup Cabeza could take the lead.

6

>> >> >>

In two sleeps, they reached the Spanish outpost. It was a jumble of thatched huts such as they had seen at the Caddo village, with one mud structure which appeared to be the headquarters building. A sentry lounged in sloppy posture against the wall at the doorway.

By heaven, thought Don Pedro, if he were a soldier of mine, he'd look alert. The old man brushed irritably past the curious sentry, followed by Cabeza and Sanchez.

A lieutenant in a soiled tunic slouched behind a desk and watched the trio curiously as their eyes adjusted to the dim light. He was not surprised. The native grapevine had brought rumors of an approaching party two days ago. He was merely puzzled as to why anyone who did not have to would spend time in this god-forsaken swelter of a gulf coast.

Don Pedro stepped forward, nodded in polite greeting, and began.

"*Buenos días, amigo.* I am Don Pedro Garcia. We

are starting on a search for my lost son. He disappeared five years ago on an expedition to the north."

The lieutenant's eyes widened. "Welcome, *Señor* Garcia, to our poor facility." He rose, offered chairs, and asked a young native girl to bring wine. These were obviously persons of importance.

Light conversation followed, questions about the sea crossing and about the quest. At last, the lieutenant began to move around to the point of the conversation.

"I am sorry, *Señor* Garcia, but I cannot allow you to cross the river. It cannot be done without the sanction of the Crown."

Don Pedro was completely unimpressed. This was no more than he had expected. It merely signaled the opening of negotiations. He glanced at Cabeza and Sanchez sitting dejected on their stools. Ah, he would demonstrate for them the art of diplomacy.

"Well, so be it," he shrugged.

"But, never mind," the lieutenant was continuing. "We will enjoy your visit while you are here. Ours is a lonely existence. We are so forgotten here on the border and so undermanned and underpaid. So drink up and we will enjoy each other's company this evening!"

He raised his glass in salute and the others did likewise.

"Ah yes," agreed Don Pedro. "Yours must be a dedicated life, to submit to such indignities. It is a shame that you cannot be adequately repaid for your loyalty to the Crown."

Almost unnoticed, a small bag of soft leather had appeared on the desk top in front of Garcia. The contents clinked softly as the old man gently poked it forward a short way with a gnarled forefinger. The lieutenant appeared to pay no attention, but continued to talk.

"Yes, we do our best. But with such few troops, what can I do?" He spread his palms in a helpless gesture. "We cannot even adequately patrol the river crossing. Why, even tomorrow, it must remain unguarded for most of the morning while we scout the lower crossing!"

Garcia saw with satisfaction that somewhere during
the exaggerated gesturing, the bag of silver had disappeared. The contract was complete.

"One of my men will show you to an area where
you may spend the night," the lieutenant was continuing. "After you are settled, we will resume our conversation. I trust you three will dine with me?"

They followed a soldier in a shabby uniform toward
an open area where their party was already preparing
camp. Cabeza was plodding along at Garcia's elbow,
puzzling over the scene just past.

"Forgive me, Don Pedro," he mused at length. "Did
the lieutenant take a bribe to allow us to cross?"

At Garcia's other albow, Sanchez snickered at the
young man's naïveté. The old don glanced at him
with irritation, then turned to Ramon.

"Of course not, lieutenant. You heard no mention
of a bribe, did you?"

"But money changed hands."

"Only a gift. A young officer in the service of the
Crown is woefully underpaid."

"But, I—"

"Cabeza," snapped Don Pedro, becoming a trifle
irritated, "you heard no mention of anything to be
done in exchange for money, did you?"

"No, *señor*."

"Very well, there is nothing more to be said."

So, there was not. The three were royally enter-
tained with the best dinner to be afforded on the
frontier and no word was said of the coming day.

Early next morning, the now-friendly young lieutenant made a big show of good-byes and wished them
a pleasant sea journey. Then he summoned his small
platoon and marched stiffly through the village street
and out of sight down the trail. There was silence in
the encampment, except for the occasional cry of one
of the native children at play.

"Come," Garcia motioned to no one in particular.
"We go."

Quickly, they packed the baggage of the expedition
and splashed across the shallow water of the ford,
heading north into the unknown. The level landscape,

dotted with scrubby trees, stretched away into shimmering distance. Don Pedro kneed his smooth-stepping mare up beside Sanchez.

"Which way?"

Sanchez had by now had time to reflect on his course of action. He had begun to remember some almost forgotten details of the previous expedition.

How could he have forgotten, he now wondered, day after day of the hot sun beating down on his back as they traveled? Of course, their primary direction had been north and the sun had swung in its merciless arc across the southern sky each day. He had started each morning with the sun on his right shoulder and had slumped exhausted at night with its coppery orb sinking into the horizon at his left. It would be easier this time on horseback.

A gust of hot wind struck his face as he turned to look at the straggling column behind. Yes, that had been the other thing. The wind had never ceased to blow, that livelong summer. Each day, the steady south breeze had struck full on their backs as they traveled.

Sanchez suddenly had a great resurgence of confidence in his ability. Of course he could lead the expedition. It required, at least for a time, only that they hold a generally northerly course. That, he could manage. He could gauge direction both by the sun's position and by the prevailing south wind at their backs. He picked out a blue hilltop in the shimmering distance. That would be their landmark for the day.

Sanchez suddenly became aware that Don Pedro had repeated his question.

"Which way, Sanchez?"

The little man was exhilarated, almost drunk with the euphoria of authority. He stood in his stirrups and, with a long, sweeping gesture, pointed at the blue shimmering hill, days to the north.

"We follow the wind!"

7

>> >> >>

Sanchez, Garcia, and Cabeza squatted on woven rush mats in the shade of a thatched arbor. Lizard was in deep conversation with leaders of the village as the others waited.

And this village was exactly like the rest, Sanchez fretted. Another few days of travel, another village of thatched huts. Garcia insisted on questioning in depth at every stop. It was stupid, Sanchez realized. The area where the young officer had been lost was weeks further to the north. Then he became irritated at himself. Mother of God, it was almost as if for a moment he had begun to believe his own story!

Why should he care that the old don wished to give his trinkets to any chance village they encountered along the way? If it helped to keep interest alive, why not let him have his way?

Sanchez sighed and scratched his back against the pole on which he leaned. Actually, he reflected, it was relatively comfortable here in the late afternoon shade. These savages built, for summer use, a sort of open-sided arbor with thatched roof. It kept the sun from beating down the livelong day, yet let the south breezes cool the sweat. Most of the cooking, much of the living, even, was carried out in these structures during the summer months. Only in rainy or chilly weather would the Caddoes retreat to the shelter of the huts.

Sanchez let his gaze wander across the level plain to the north. It seemed to stretch to the end of the earth and Sanchez began to wonder if he had made a mistake. He had had no idea, at the beginning, how persistent Don Pedro Garcia could be. He had thought in terms of leading the expedition aimlessly for a time, until the old man became discouraged and began to tire. At that point, they could all go home, everyone richer except the *Señor* Garcia, who had more wealth than he needed anyway.

Somehow, it had not worked out that way at all. He, Sanchez, was becoming discouraged and tired. Don Pedro, on the other hand, appeared younger and more vigorous than at the start. He was thriving on this life. The first time Sanchez had seen the old don, he had appeared just that. A tired old aristocrat, limping from ancient battle wounds and arthritis and mourning the loss of his only son.

Now old Garcia seemed decades younger. To observe him from a distance, as he sat the gray mare with military bearing, one would think of him as a soldier in the prime of life. There was no indication that he had any intention of backing down from this search until his mission was resolved. It seemed that he fully expected to find evidence of his son, either alive, or firm proof of his death.

Sanchez exhaled a sigh of frustration. What if no evidence were ever found? Would the old man continue to press to the north until they all died in the unknown land? Just how far, Sanchez wondered, could one travel to the north? Might they not be trapped in a climate impossible for survival as winter descended? If worst came to worst, he wondered if there were enough men who could be counted on to mutiny and refuse to throw their lives away.

He was afraid not. The expedition seemed a tight-knit, loyal, and enthusiastic unit. The lancers, hand-picked by Lieutenant Cabeza, seemed to take so much pride in their platoon that it appeared they would follow their young officer into hell itself. The cross-bowmen, well-paid professional soldiers, likewise seemed proud of their position with the expedition. As for the others, most were Garcia family servants. Some had been with the Garcias for generations and would undoubtedly die for the old don if it were requested.

Sanchez was always alert for an alternative course of action which would allow him flexibility in case he saw opportunity. This was his entire way of survival —to change loyalties when it seemed profitable. His frustration now was based largely on the fact that his choices were so limited. The reluctant scoundrel was being carried along on the crest of a wave of loyalty and enthusiasm. How very odd that everyone else in the party shared this feeling, when the whole mission had been the creation of Sanchez in the first place.

He glanced over at the conversation in progress between Lizard and the chief squatting across from him. Suddenly, all his attention was focused on the two. The chief was gesturing and nodding eagerly, pointing northward and holding up his spread fingers.

Don Pedro leaned forward and spoke sharply to Sanchez.

"What does he say?"

Lizard was listening intently to the rapidly talking native. After what seemed an eternity, he turned to the others, a look of mixed wonderment and pleasure on his face.

"Him say yes, hair-face boy! Big medicine." He pointed to the north. "Him six, maybe seven sleeps."

Garcia was bubbling over with questions and, for some time, the awkward conversation continued. Actually, little new information was gained. The basic message was the original one.

A few days' travel to the north, there was apparently a village where a young hair-faced man lived. He was regarded with special honor of some sort. Beyond that information, the conversation was limited, both by language problems and by lack of any actual knowledge on the part of their informants. The story was mostly hearsay. There was apparently no one in this village who had actually seen the hair-face. They had only heard rumors.

Nevertheless, Don Pedro Garcia was convinced that the young man they told of would prove to be his son. He could hardly wait to begin the next day's travel.

Sanchez was not so certain. There was something here that did not ring true. The entire thing was too easy. Certainly, the story told by these savages fit precisely that which he had fabricated for the old don. That bothered him considerably to start with. How could any set of actual facts coincide with the series of falsehoods which came entirely from his own imagination? He shook his head in bewilderment.

The others could not understand the hesitance of Sanchez. The entire membership of the Garcia expedition was jubilant. The slim chance that had led the party halfway around the world was about to pay off. Ah, the honor that would be their lot if the mission were a success. Some possibly even thought of the generosity of Don Pedro. His gratitude toward those who had taken part in the rescue of his son would be beyond belief.

Under normal circumstances, those would have been the thoughts of Sanchez. But not now. His confused thoughts seemed to whirl in his head. Sanchez had to get away to think.

He walked a little way from the village, moving aimlessly, but in the general direction of their travel. A jumble of rock gleamed whitish in the pale twilight and he stopped to sit. Behind him in the village, Sanchez could hear the revelry. Don Pedro had ordered a ration of wine for all and spirits were high.

This was probably the first time in history that Sanchez had missed an opportunity for free wine. He even neglected to seek female companionship as he usually did during these night stops. This fact reaffirmed the seriousness of this thought as he watched the dusk deepen and the stars begin to appear. The breeze at his back was not unpleasant and it was good to be alone to collect his thoughts. He watched the sky in the north until the Pole Star appeared.

Mother of God, Sanchez thought, how is it that everyone believes my story but me?

There could be no chance that this might be the son of Don Pedro Garcia, could there? He had been lost many weeks further north. But the natives had said, through Lizard, the interpreter, that this young hair-faced person was "big medicine." Certainly, it seemed reasonable that the son of Don Pedro, if alive, would be the recipient of honor of some sort.

A soft step behind him brought Sanchez to his feet with a start. Ramon Cabeza stepped out of the dusk and motioned the other to resume his seat. He joined him on a nearby rock.

"Sanchez, you are troubled."

It was a statement, not a question.

"Oh no, *señor*," Sanchez whined, adopting his groveling peon attitude. "I only—"

"Stop!" Cabeza waved him to silence impatiently. "I mean you no trouble."

There was a long silence while Sanchez waited uneasily. What could the young lieutenant want? At last, the younger man spoke again.

"Sanchez, you and I are very different, but I think we want the same thing."

Sanchez was startled. Was the scrupulously loyal officer of lancers ruled by greed, also?

"We want only the best for Don Pedro Garcia," Cabeza continued.

Ah yes, thought Sanchez. It is not that he is a scoundrel, but that he trusts me to be as honest as he. And that is good. When one trusts you, he is easier to deceive.

"None of us have been as far north as this, except

you. And you are troubled. What is it, Sanchez? Do you doubt this story we have heard today?"

Something about an honest question with no ulterior motive made Sanchez give an honest answer. He dropped the fawning attitude and spoke straight to the other, man-to-man.

"I do not know, señor. The story is right, but the place is wrong. It should be many weeks to the north."

"Many weeks?" The other was incredulous. "How big is this country?"

Sanchez spread his hands in a gesture of helplessness.

"Who knows? I only know that we traveled many weeks to get to the place where the young Garcia was lost."

He paused, confused. He had nearly admitted to the young officer that he did not actually know where they were going. He tried to assume a more knowledgeable air.

"The savages there live in a different sort of house, a tent made of leather. They hunt the humpbacked cattle for food."

Cabeza nodded. He had heard of the shaggy buffalo, but they had seen only a few scattered herds at a distance. It was still difficult for him to comprehend the vastness of the prairie ahead.

"Very well. But whether this is the one we seek or not, I will count on you. I will not have Don Pedro hurt if we can avoid it."

There was only a hint of a veiled threat, which indicated the young officer not quite as naïve as Sanchez had thought. But there was also the sincere request, the asking of cooperation from an individual who, by implication, Cabeza was approaching as an equal. The implied approval was almost more than Sanchez could bear. He swelled with pride.

"Of course, señor."

8
>> >> >>

The "six, maybe seven" sleeps mentioned by the savages were to be cut to five, according to Garcia. He wished to spare neither horses nor men as they pushed rapidly ahead.

They encountered one other village after two "sleeps" and, on questioning, received the same story. Yes, there was such a hair-face. Many of the people in this village had seen and talked to him. Beyond that information, the conversation bogged down again in the everpresent language difficulty. Again, however, there was the mention that the hair-faced one was honored. They spent the night and forged rapidly onward next day.

Apparently, the village they sought was somewhat larger than most. The trail was well traveled and seemed plainer and broader as they came closer to their destination. Smaller paths straggled in through the brushy plain and from the canebrakes along the streams, joining the main pathway. It reminded Sanchez of a river, growing in size as it was joined by smaller tributaries along its course.

It was shortly after noon on the day they all anticipated, when they encountered two young natives with bows and arrows, hunting rabbits. The two were fearful at first, but Lizard was able to set them at ease.

Yes, the village was ahead. Word had preceded the party and they were expected, but their motives were apparently suspect. To reassure the savages, Garcia gave them some small gifts and asked that they go ahead to their village. The two nodded, pleased. They loped out of sight down the trail at the peculiar jogtrot that seemed the normal gait for long distances among these people.

Shadows were lengthening before it began to be apparent that they were approaching the village. A smoky haze from cooking fires hung over a shallow valley ahead. Soon curious people ventured out to meet the travelers, walking alongside the horses and jabbering excitedly to each other. Lizard talked back to them, in his glory as interpreter for the expedition.

They threaded their way down the main path between scattered huts and approached a knot of men who appeared to be leaders of the encampment. Lizard conversed with them briefly, then turned, pointing to one of the men.

"Him chief. Hair-face there." He indicated one of the long council houses nearby.

The man identified as chief proudly led the way to the council house and beckoned them inside. The others stepped back in deference to Don Pedro and the old man stooped to enter. Cabeza and Sanchez followed. The chief beckoned again and pointed to the far end of the shadowy room.

Their eyes adjusted slowly to the dimness. A recumbent figure lay on a rush mat, rising to an elbow to greet them.

"Hair-face!" said Lizard proudly.

The object of their gaze was a boy of some thirteen or fourteen years, a scruffy fringe of beard sprouting along his jaw and upper lip. Flat-lidded eyes and a vacant stare gave evidence to mental deficiency. Saliva drooled from the corner of his mouth, which spread in a blank, childlike grin.

In silence, the travelers stared. Was this pitiful animal-like creature that on which the hopes of Don Pedro Garcia had been focused? This could not be the lost Garcia heir. This was hardly more than a child, a half-breed probably, and obviously an idiot.

Sanchez finally realized the truth. The "big medicine" so proudly mentioned by poor Lizard must have to do with a curious custom among the savages. Madmen and lunatics, he had heard, were thought to be possessed of spirits. Therefore, to avoid angering the spirits, such unfortunates were treated with great deference and protected from all harm.

"Mother of God!" Sanchez whispered, crossing himself.

"Sanchez!" Garcia roared.

The idiot boy on the mat jumped in fright and began to cry at the noise. Garcia whirled and grasped the cowering Sanchez by the front of his tunic.

"Son of a snake!" The old don's voice trembled with rage. "For this you drag me halfway around the earth?"

Don Pedro's great sword came whispering out of its scabbard, gleaming dully in the dim light. Sanchez squealed in terror and fell to his knees, squeezing his eyes tightly shut to avoid watching the final blow descend.

"Stop!" The clear voice of Cabeza rang across the room. "It is not his fault, Señor Garcia!"

The young lieutenant stepped quickly between the two to plead with the distraught old man.

"Please, señor, Sanchez has said it was not here. The place would be much further north."

Sanchez, white-faced, dared to open his eyes and nod in frantic agreement. He was still unable to speak. Cabeza continued, somehow sensing that the flow of words was staying the old man's hand.

"He tells of a different people, who live in leather tents and hunt the wild cattle. And, señor," his voice lowered and became confidential, "if you kill him, who is there to lead us to that place?"

His eyes still fixed on the cowering Sanchez, Don Pedro sheathed his sword. He whirled on his heel without a word and strode stiffly from the lodge. Sanchez, still on his knees and too weak to rise, made little gasping noises. Cabeza helped him to his feet.

"Him not hair-face?" Lizard was completely bewildered by this exciting turn of events.

"Not same hair-face. Wrong hair-face!" Cabeza attempted explanation, since Sanchez was still not able to communicate. Obviously, Lizard still did not fully understand. Cabeza was not certain that he himself did. The visitors filed outside into the early evening.

Don Pedro was nowhere to be seen. In his absence, Ramon Cabeza gave orders to camp for the night. It was a strained evening. At every motion or sound, Sanchez jumped in terror, fearful that Don Pedro would return with his sword.

Eventually, after full darkness, the old don did return. He spoke to no one, but sought his sleeping blankets. Sanchez came out of temporary hiding and the camp began to settle down for the night.

To smooth over the incident, Cabeza took it on himself to take gifts to the leaders of the village, with a special gift of a mirror for the unfortunate boy who was the center of all the misunderstanding. Sanchez had recovered to the extent that he was able to accompany the lieutenant and Lizard and assist in the giving of the presents and the attempted explanations.

Sanchez had been convinced that he was as good as dead and it had been a very sobering experience. Yet, there was another experience which was equally mind-boggling. Ramon Cabeza had saved his life. It was the first time in his memory that anyone had intervened on his behalf—in anything.

More puzzling to the devious mind of Sanchez was the reason. Why had Cabeza done such a thing, when he obviously had nothing to gain? Sanchez had felt, since their conversation a few nights ago, that the lieutenant had evaluated him quite accurately. There

was little to make him believe that Cabeza respected
him or even liked him very much. Cabeza was merely
willing to tolerate and cooperate with him if it would
be helpful to the *Señor* Garcia's quest.

Ah yes, that must be it. Cabeza knew that the
search depended on the memory of Sanchez. Almost
forgotten was the uneasy thought that the lieutenant
half-suspected the truth. The fact that Sanchez did
not know where he was leading them must have
crossed the quick mind of Ramon Cabeza.

For now, Sanchez was happy merely to be alive. Let
tomorrow take care of itself.

The morning did come, of course. Everyone in the
party was tense and uneasy, wondering which direction they would take. Don Pedro still spoke to no one.
Would he now turn back, having failed in his quest?
Even Cabeza was reluctant to bring up the subject. He
elected to wait until time to start the day's march.

Sanchez avoided Don Pedro as long as possible, but
eventually, as it came time to mount up, the two had
to make contact. The old don stepped into the stirrup
and straightened himself, ramrod-stiff in the saddle.
He glanced over the assembling column. It was no-
ticeable that his face was drawn. Don Pedro Garcia
had spent a sleepless night.

His steely gaze fell on the still-frightened Sanchez
for a long moment. When he spoke, his voice was
almost gentle in its quiet tones.

"Well, Sanchez, which way now?"

9
>> >> >>

Cabeza had done some very deep thinking as a result of the incident just past. There had come a sense of responsibility that he felt forced upon him. At the beginning of the expedition, he had envisioned himself as merely an officer of lancers. The party was under command of the *Señor* Garcia, for whom he had complete respect and loyalty. It would be guided by Sanchez, whose job it was to show the way, regardless of what anyone else thought of him as a person.

Now, Cabeza was forced to re-evaluate his own position. The incident back in the Caddo village had made a number of facts quite clear. Don Pedro could easily become unstable enough to exhibit poor judgment. In addition, he was, after all, an old man. He could easily fall victim to an illness or accident. Then he, Ramon Cabeza, would have to assume command of the party, because there was no one else to do so. Somehow, Cabeza had overlooked this fact. He had grown up with the image of the elder Garcia before him as an invincible figure. It was with a great deal of misgiving that he thought of attempting to fill such mighty boots.

And then there was Sanchez. Cabeza suspected, of course, that the devious little man had very little knowledge of where he was leading them. Despite this, Sanchez's story had been accurate thus far. Cabeza was inclined to listen to him, though not to trust him to any extent.

He now realized, however, that if anything happened to Sanchez, as it nearly had last night, that they would be in a strange country without a guide.

Perhaps Lizard could be of help—if he could talk to him. Would it be possible to learn the language of the other? It seemed too difficult a task. He noticed, however, that when Lizard conversed with Sanchez, he always used many exaggerated gestures.

Cabeza asked Sanchez about this as they rode.

"Who knows?" shrugged Sanchez. "They talk with their hands."

So the gesturing had no significance, at least to Sanchez. The lieutenant thought it over more fully and was still certain that something had meaning. Lizard, he recalled, whenever he used the term "hair-face," always accompanied the words with a motion of his hand along his jaw. Cabeza determined to try an experiment.

During the noon halt, he managed to sit near Lizard. He still wondered exactly how he would accomplish this. Then he noticed a lancer near them who had a full beard. It was a magnificent brush, actually something of a legend among the lancers. Cabeza caught Lizard's eye, pointed to the dozing lancer, and made the little hand motion along the jaw. Lizard looked startled, then burst into laughter, nodding vigorously.

"Hair-face! *Big* hair-face!"

As he said the words, Lizard repeated the hand sign, adding a gesture that could only be translated as "big."

Aha, thought Cabeza. It *is* a hand sign thing. He must learn more. He picked up his waterskin and took a sip, then offered it to Lizard with a gesture he hoped would be interpreted as a question. The other nodded, pointed to the stream nearby, and made a hand sign with a fluttering, flowing motion of the fingers. Of course! "Water."

By the time they resumed travel, Cabeza understood the signs for several common words. He was elated, but probably no more so than Lizard. The young native was eager to show him more signs.

Sanchez, of course, was irritable and moody. He resented the fact that, suddenly, Cabeza could communicate with their interpreter better than he. In addition, both were obviously enjoying it.

As the days passed and the party traveled further north, Cabeza became more adept at the use of the signs. He was constantly amazed at the breadth of ideas that could be transmitted in this way.

After many sleeps, the travelers had entered a gradually changing landscape; the plain was more rolling, the grasses taller. In some areas, there were sizable valleys and hillsides covered with trees, most of which appeared to be various species of oaks. At one vantage point where they paused for a noon rest, it was possible to see for great distances in any direction. With this advantage, it was apparent that there was a rather abrupt line running in the general direction of their travel. To the east of this wavering margin were the tree-covered hills and valleys. To the west stretched the rolling plain, as far as the eye could see, finally becoming lost in the blue of distance. The party swung slightly to the west for easier traveling in the grassland when the march resumed.

It was toward evening of the same day that they sighted the smoke of a village ahead. To the travelers' surprise, the dwellings were completely different from the thatched square houses of the Caddoes. These were grass structures, but shaped like beehives in appearance, with pointed tops.

Lizard approached some of the inhabitants and, in due time, the party was ushered forward to a larger structure in the center of the village. This, they assumed, was this group's version of the council house.

Cabeza was uneasy about entering. The openings, one on each side, were only waist-high. His military mind rebelled at the idea of entering practically on all fours in a completely defenseless stance. He managed to step quickly through and straighten as rapidly as possible. He glanced around the large circular room but found nothing threatening. The entrances were well planned for defense, he conceded. Any enemy must enter one at a time—and in a defenseless position. The major threat to the defenders would be that the attackers could use fire. The dry grass thatch would be terribly vulnerable.

The visitors were seated on the white clay floor across from the leaders of the village and a parlay began. Lizard explained their mission and the usual small gifts were distributed.

It was at about this time that Cabeza made a startling observation. Most of the dialogue was carried on in the sign language. As he observed further, it became apparent that Lizard spoke very little of the language of these savages. Likewise, they understood little of his.

It had not occurred to the young lieutenant that here was an entirely different nation, with not only different dwellings, but different customs and language. Then the people of the skin tents as described by Sanchez must be yet another group, with their own language.

Cabeza's most significant observation, however, was that he was able to understand much of the dialogue in sign talk. How valuable, he immediately recognized, to be able to communicate with various tribes they encountered. He resolved to observe closely and master the skill, with the help of Lizard.

Yes, the village chiefs were signing, they had seen Hairfaces before. No, they knew of none living with the natives. They had been only passing through.

For some reason, it seemed that Don Pedro was now less impatient than before his great disappointment. He seemed willing to accept the statements of the natives at face value. At least, they knew of Hairfaces.

This proved that some Spaniards had previously traveled this way. One of these could easily have been Juan Garcia.

Perhaps it was only that the contact with a new and different tribe signified progress to the travelers. Whatever the reason, as they settled in for the night, there was a new feeling of optimism in their encampment.

10
>> >> >>

Sanchez brooded over the obvious delight that Lizard was exhibiting in teaching the sign talk. Cabeza was quick to learn and soon could understand most of the exchange between the interpreter and the leaders of various groups they encountered.

However, the lieutenant sensed that Sanchez resented his intrusion. He elected to remain aloof during the parlays with the natives. It was more expedient at times anyway for the other party to be unaware that one of the Hairfaces understood their sign talk.

One wizened chief went so far as to approach Lizard with a suggestion that they could contrive together to defraud the travelers out of more gifts and trinkets. Lizard was appropriately indignant, but the spectacular response was on the part of Cabeza. The lieutenant had caught enough of the drift of talk to recognize the attempt at subterfuge. He rose haughtily and, ignoring the chief, spoke in sign talk directly to Lizard.

"Come! We will waste no talk with this fool!"

He turned on his heel and left the parlay, while the faces of the natives remained frozen in shocked surprise.

It was noted at the next village that there was a great deal of deference to the travelers. They had long since realized that word was preceding them, telling of their coming. There was some discussion around the campfire as to how this might be accomplished. Some thought the native drums might echo a message, others that it was done with smoke signals. They had seen both during their travels.

Finally, Cabeza realized what should have been obvious all along. They could ask Lizard. With a combination of signs and Spanish, he broached the question. Lizard shrugged, as if the answer should be obvious.

"Men run ahead!"

The party laughed uproariously. The mood was good. It had remained optimistic since Don Pedro's change of attitude at the first of the beehive villages. Now the old don was very nearly his enthusiastic self again. He seemed to have accepted the fact that there would be many weeks of travel and search.

Sanchez still carefully concealed the fact that he had no clear idea of their direction. He was beginning to be painfully aware of the fact that a showdown might ultimately be necessary. To cover his subterfuge, he pretended to recognize landmarks. He would stare at a uniquely shaped hill in the distance and nod, as if to himself, in satisfaction.

In actuality, he recognized nothing at all. He had paid no attention to direction, even, on his previous expedition. One hill or grove or stream looked pretty much like another to him. He did take pains to keep the south wind at their backs and to keep pointing north. The country was greener and more pleasant here, which increased the general mood of optimism.

They now saw more herds of the strange hump-backed cattle and the herds were larger. The animals showed no fear, but only raised shaggy heads to stare curiously as they passed. Sanchez described, during a noon halt, how the lancers on the previous expedition had delighted in hunting the animals. He recalled that they had furnished much meat for the party.

The lancers needed little encouragement. Before the evening halt, they had secured a fat young cow. That evening, the gentle warm breeze was scented with the sweet aroma of broiling buffalo hump. Sanchez, though remembering little of practical use, had retained the memory that this was the choicest of cuts. The others readily agreed and the entire party gorged themselves on the rich meat.

Next day, they encountered another new experience. A village, seen from afar by the pall of smoke hanging over the area, proved to be that of yet another tribe. These people lived in a sort of half-buried house, partly in and partly above the ground. The exposed portion appeared to be constructed of poles and brush.

These natives were also cultivating fields of maize, pumpkins, and a sort of bean. They were called the Growers, Lizard informed the others. He had heard of them, though he did not understand their language.

The Growers proved to be a very hospitable people. They carried on a system of trade with other tribes, it appeared, exchanging the products of their agriculture for meat and skins from the hunting tribes.

"Ask them more of the hunters," urged Cabeza. It was becoming apparent that the nomadic people of the skin tents described by Sanchez would be hunters.

Yes, came the answer, without hesitation. There were several groups. The Growers traded indiscriminately with them all, though there was often war between the different tribes of hunters.

Was there any among them with hair on the face?

The Growers conversed among themselves for a time, then one answered, using sign talk.

They had seen no hair-face, but there was said to be one, much further north. He was a mighty chief, it was said, hated by his enemies. There was a tale that he had met in combat with Gray Wolf, a great chief of the tribe known as Head Splitters. The hair-faced one had killed Gray Wolf, bringing much prestige to his own people.

Where could more be learned? The Growers were unanimous on this point. To the north!

Now even Sanchez was excited. He had completely forgotten that he had originally considered this a useless fiasco, designed only for his own possible enrichment. Sanchez was now as convinced as anyone that it might be possible to find Juan Garcia.

Cabeza, for his part, was concerned with so much optimism. He remembered only too well the near tragedy that had resulted from the last disappointment. Don Pedro, it could be clearly seen, was burning with eagerness again. The old man was restless, anxious to be on the way. This time, surely, their search would meet with success, his entire attitude seemed to say.

The lieutenant sought him out during the long twilight of the prairie evening.

"*Señor* Garcia," he began hesitantly, "you know that it may not be your son."

"Of course, my boy!" Don Pedro's enthusiasm still bubbled. "But it may be! They said this man is a great leader!" He whacked the younger man affectionately across the shoulders. "Do not worry, Ramon! We shall go and see!"

The old don's eyes sparkled in the firelight and his excited smile spread across the weather-beaten face. Tonight, Cabeza thought, Don Pedro looked years younger. It was little short of amazing, how much difference it made to have something to look forward to.

Cabeza was still disturbed, however. There was actually very little chance that this legendary chief further north was even a Spaniard, much less one particular Spaniard, the son of Don Pedro Garcia. And, after further weeks of penetration into the heart of the continent, what if they found nothing? Or the wrong man? Could the stamina of Don Pedro withstand another disappointment of this kind?

Cabeza sighed and turned, sleepless, in his blankets. Things had seemed so much simpler at the start of the expedition, before he assigned himself the responsibility he now felt. Why couldn't he have merely been able to carry out his duties as head of the expedition's military unit? Things had a way of becoming so complicated out in the real world, away from the cloistered influence of his home and of the Academy.

Now, he muttered to himself, he had come to the point where he felt a responsibility not only to Don Pedro, but to Sanchez and the whole damned company.

What triumphs, terrors, or defeats might lie ahead between their present camp and the trail that led toward the Pole Star, winking brightly in the northern sky? At last, tired from the day's travel, he drifted into troubled sleep.

Nothing worthy of note occurred for a few days. The party rose, traveled, made camp, ate, and slept, and the distance slipped slowly behind them, one day much the same as the one before. They encountered no more villages.

Occasionally, the lancers procured a buffalo and everyone ate well for a day. They had slipped into a comfortable routine.

Don Pedro was becoming restless, almost irritable at the lack of any apparent progress. Then, one evening as they made camp, an astonishing event caught the attention of the entire party.

Three young natives approached the encampment. Their dusty garments showed evidence of long travel. Cautiously, they advanced, repeatedly making the open-palm sign for peace. Lizard moved forward to communicate.

The newcomers were Growers, they stated. They had heard of the searching party and had traveled several sleeps to meet them. It was said that Hairfaces would exchange gifts for information they sought and it was for this purpose they had come.

"They have knowledge of my son?" Don Pedro asked eagerly.

Lizard shook his head.

"No. Have big medicine. Hair-face medicine!"

He pointed to a shapeless bundle that one of the natives carried.

"Him want trade."

Slowly, almost reverently, the man unwrapped his bundle.

"Him trade from hunter tribes," Lizard was explaining.

The last leather wrapping slipped away and a round object gleamed dully in the firelight. Proudly, the native placed the thing in the hands of the shaken Don Pedro.

It was rusty and dented, but identifiable at a glance. Oddly out of place, the artifact was completely foreign to the prairies of New Spain. It was a battered and well-used accoutrement of another world, an old-fashioned Spanish military helmet.

11

» » »

It was hours later and the party was quieting for the night. Don Pedro Garcia still sat by the fire, holding the helmet in his lap. He had eaten not a bite and had spoken hardly a word to anyone. Since the finding of the helmet, he had spent most of the time busily scouring the object with sand, cleaning and polishing it. His gnarled old fingers moved lovingly, almost reverently, over the now-shiny surface. From time to time, he ran his thumb nail along a deep nick in the upturned brim and a corresponding groove in the smooth curve.

Cabeza, concerned over the old man's preoccupation, sauntered over to sit beside him. Don Pedro did not even look up, but after a long moment began to speak softly, feeling the groove along the left side of the helmet.

"It was in the south of France," he related, almost to himself, as if unaware that he had a listener. "The man was big, very big for a Frenchman, but he was

quick. He dodged under my stroke and nearly killed
me. The helmet saved me, but the armorer could
never polish the scar out of it."

He fingered the deep groove again.

Slowly, the significance of the half-forgotten story
sank into the consciousness of Cabeza.

"You mean, *señor*, *this* is the helmet?"

Sanchez had joined them and the story now became
clear to him, also.

"Yes, *Señor* Cabeza, the young Officer Garcia wore
his father's armor!"

Slowly, Don Pedro turned, the look of wonder still
on his face. He stared at Sanchez as if he had never
seen him before.

"Sanchez, at times I have thought you were a liar.
You still may be, but I have trusted you because it
was all I had. Now this," he held up the helmet,
"proves you told some truth."

Sanchez was almost overcome by the approval he
was receiving. He was uneasy, however. The presence
of the helmet worn by the young Juan Garcia proved
nothing. He might be dead. Someone else might have
carried the helmet halfway across the continent to
this spot.

Yet, it was easy to be optimistic. This terrain did
look remarkably like that in which the young officer
had been lost. Hope continued to grow in the mind of
Sanchez. It would be a wonderful thing if the son of
Don Pedro could be found. With a sudden start, he
realized that he was hoping for something without
thinking of the financial return for himself. What a
strange feeling. Perhaps he was becoming addled from
too much time in the hot sun.

"*Señor*," Cabeza was protesting mildly, "this does
not mean that he is alive."

"I know, Ramon." Something like a tear glistened
in the old man's eye. "But I wish to know. And he did
come this way!"

It was only a few days later that they sighted riders
in the distance. There were perhaps a score of men,
sweeping confidently across the plain. The two par-

ties saw each other at approximately the same moment and the strangers altered course to approach
slowly and with caution.

The travelers had seen horses used by the natives,
mostly as pack animals. These were ridden. Don Pedro, with an old campaigner's eye, sized up the approaching contingent. The savages appeared to be
experienced horsemen. What few natives they had
seen on horseback previously were poor riders, seated
too far back and clumsy in their handling of the
animals.

These men, on the contrary, sat well forward on
the withers and exhibited good control. They appeared
to be of a different bone structure than the natives
previously seen, also. They were muscular in appearance, with longer facial features and high cheekbones.
All were heavily armed.

Three of the newcomers detached themselves from
the rest of the party and rode slowly forward. The
man in the middle, a leader by his bearing and de-
meanor, held his right hand up, with open palm forward.
The travelers had begun to recognize this as the signal
for an invitation to talk.

Dun Pedro pointed to Sanchez, Cabeza, and Lizard.
They advanced cautiously to meet the newcomers
halfway. Lizard, the only one on foot, walked proudly
beside the old don's horse, with Sanchez on his other
side. They stopped at a conversational distance and
the sign talk began. Cabeza followed it closely.

"We have traveled far. We have gifts and we wish to
ask questions."

The other chief nodded stiffly.

"How are you called?"

"I am Lizard. These are men from across the Big
Water. We look for the son of our chief."

He indicated the elder Garcia.

Garcia, thinking to help explain the situation, drew
the helmet from his saddlebag and held it up.

"*Aiee!*" exclaimed one of the warriors. The three
began an animated conversation among themselves.

At last, Lizard interrupted them to ask another question.

"You have seen a man with hairy face?"

The three glanced uneasily at each other. Another animated conversation ensued. Finally, the leader turned and signed back.

"We may be able to help you. You must come to our camp."

There was now the interpretation and discussion among the Garcia party and tentative agreement.

"Ask who they are," Cabeza suggested. "They must be one of the hunter tribes."

"How are you called?" signed Lizard.

"I am Lean Bull. Come with us. You spoke of gifts?"

Lizard translated and Garcia turned to call forward one of the servants with a pack of trade goods. Some small trinkets were presented, to the obvious pleasure of the warriors.

At length, the two groups moved on together, each party of armed men still somewhat suspicious of the other. They moved in two parallel files, a few paces apart. The lancers eyed their native counterparts and the savages returned the attention.

Cabeza was interested in the equipment of the other group. Long lances bristled along the column. They appeared much like those of his own men, except for the stone lance points. Other men carried short, heavy bows and quivers of arrows. It was some time before he noticed that at the waist of nearly every man hung a war club. The implement consisted of a stone the size of a man's fist, bound into a handle of wood, somewhat like an ax. It appeared to be a formidable weapon.

The combined party traveled for nearly half the afternoon across rolling prairie and flat-topped hills. Herds of buffalo, their brown color appearing black in the distance, dotted the plain. Finally, topping a long ridge, the group looked over a vast basin in the prairie. Through the center of the lush, grassy meadows meandered a stream, marked by a darker green fringe of trees. In places, one or two huge old cottonwoods stood like sentinels presiding over the course of the stream.

Lean Bull, leader of the savages, stopped his horse and pointed across the valley. There, in the haze of distance, the travelers could see smoke along the stream. The source seemed to be a cluster of dwellings. Nearby, a scattered herd of horses grazed.

Cabeza stood in his stirrups to obtain a better look. A slight change in the breeze cleared some of the smoky haze for a moment and he could catch a glimpse of the structures in the village. They were conical in shape, sharply pointed on top, with smoke rising lazily from the apex of the cone.

It took a long moment for the significance of the scene to sink into Cabeza's consciousness. These were the leather-tent people of Sanchez's stories.

Another thought occurred to the young lieutenant as the party started down the rocky hillside. He waited until they reached easier terrain in the meadow, then caught the attention of one of the savages who was riding near him. He indicated a wish to converse in the sign talk and the other nodded.

"How are your people called?" gestured Cabeza, by way of conversation.

The warrior reached down and lifted the heavy war club dangling below his waist. He cheerfully held it out for the inspection of the other.

"Our enemies call us the Head Splitters."

12
>> >> >>

That night, under cover of darkness, in an area a few days' travel away, three men and a woman gathered in the dense timber along a stream. It was hardly more than a long bow shot from their village.

Most of the People slept, but for these, the meeting must be of utmost importance.

"Where are they now?" asked Coyote.

The messenger was stripping the saddle pad and rawhide war bridle from his tired horse. He turned the animal loose and gave a parting slap on its flank, the hair stiff from drying sweat. They had covered much distance this day. He stepped over to squat on the ground and the others did likewise.

"They met the Head Splitters today. They stay tonight with them on Walnut Creek, maybe two sleeps from here."

The others nodded.

"Which way do they go?" asked Big Footed Woman.

"North. They should not find us at all."

Again, they all nodded with satisfaction.

"It was good, White Buffalo, that we moved as we did."

The medicine man accepted the compliment in silence, no less pleased. It had been his suggestion, when the rumor of a party of Hairfaces on the plains had first been heard.

The People had become affluent and successful under the leadership of a young outsider. He had, in the few short seasons with them, helped to change their way of living. He brought the horse and, with the improved methods of hunting buffalo, the People prospered. The children were fat and the women were happy. There were jokes that the Moon of Hunger, in late winter, needed a new name, for there was now food in plenty.

In addition, the People had, for the first time, successfully defended themselves in battle against the traditional enemies, the Head Splitters. This success had increased their pride as well as their prestige.

And then, the leader of the Southern band of the People had been killed in battle. The young warriors had rallied around their young leader, the hair-faced outsider who had instructed them in the skills of the horse and lance. He had married into the tribe and it was with pride that the People claimed Heads Off as one of their own and chief of the Southern band, now called the Elk-dog band.

It was still a source of amusement, the way their chief had received his name. The scouts of the People had found him, injured and lost, on the prairie. As the stranger sat up and removed his helmet, it had appeared to the onlookers, unfamiliar with that sort of headgear, that he had removed his head. It was Coyote, little dreaming that the stranger would be his son-in-law, who had dubbed him Heads Off.

Now, a few years later, all the advances of the People were threatened. According to rumors spread from one tribe to another, a column of the hair-faced ones was marching again from the south. Their purpose was unknown.

Fortunately, the scout who first heard of the matter from the Growers had become uneasy about the story. He had reported to Coyote, rather than to his chief.

"What does this mean, uncle?" The young man used the term of respect for any adult male of the People.

"I do not know, Standing Bird, but we must be very careful. Come, we will talk to White Buffalo." Surely, the medicine man would have words of wisdom.

They found the old man relaxing on his willow back rest in front of his lodge. He, too, was concerned with the rumor. He recalled that for many moons after Heads Off had joined the People, his greatest wish was to return to his own tribe. Circumstances of one sort or another had prevented his departure. But now times were more stable. Might Heads Off not decide that it would be expedient to leave?

"It is not as great a risk what the Hairfaces will do, as what Heads Off will do."

The others agreed. After much quiet discussion, a plan of action was outlined. The chief must be prevented from knowing of the expedition of outsiders. Thus, he would be unable to join them.

To this end, extra scouts would be deployed. Standing Bird, leader of the Elk-dog Warrior Society, would handle that end. The Elk-dogs, young men of unquestioned loyalty, would be informed of the crisis. Any information they acquired would be reported directly to White Buffalo. The medicine man could then advise a move to a new camp, in an area less likely to encounter the Hairfaces.

Only one move had been necessary. White Buffalo's visions had indicated that a change to an area two sleeps to the east would bring better hunting and it had been accomplished.

Coyote's heart was heavy over the necessity to deceive his son-in-law. They had shared thoughts since they first learned to communicate. The paunchy little man had come to respect and love the outsider, now a member of Coyote's own family. For these very reasons, it was necessary to take precautions to see that he was not lost. Neither the family of Heads Off, now including two sons, nor the People as a whole, could afford to be without his leadership. It was with regret, then, that Coyote was willing to compromise his usual integrity for the greater cause.

"Is anything more known of their purpose?" he now asked Standing Bird.

The young warrior shook his head.

"Among the Growers, they seek a hair-face and ask if a certain one has been seen. Who knows what they say to Head Splitters?"

Coyote chuckled the little high-pitched laugh that had long ago earned him his name. It was reminiscent of that animal's night cry on the hills behind the camp.

"*Aiee!* Would they ask Head Splitters of Hairfaces?"

The others laughed softly. Since the time of the Great Battle, when Heads Off had defeated Gray Wolf, the Head Splitters had considered him the cause of all their troubles. It was said that there were many warriors among that tribe who would gladly die at any time if they could take the hated Heads Off with them. Among the Head Splitters, he was known as Hair Face, which struck Coyote as a delightful little joke. The party of outsiders would be asking the Head Splitters about their worst enemy, by name, but without knowing it. Coyote wished he could be there to observe the looks on their faces.

This could be a very good thing. If the Head Splitters overreacted to being asked about Hair Face by Hairfaces, the two groups might easily come to battle. How fortunate, if this new threat to the People were to be wiped out by the worst enemy of the People.

Of course, there was risk involved. It could happen that the two enemies of the People would strike an agreement. The Head Splitters might tell the newcomers where the hair-face was to be found, hoping that they would take him away with them. *Aiee*, it became confusing. They must especially watch the actions of the invading party now.

The conspirators separated, re-entering the camp

from different directions. Heads Off, half asleep, happened to glance past the door flap to see his wife's parents slip back to their lodge. He smiled to himself. An incurable romantic, that Coyote. They had probably slipped off for an interlude away from the children in their lodge.

Heads Off rolled over in the sleeping robes and cuddled against the warm body of Tall One. Their own children were too small to become that sort of problem yet. He would worry about that later. For now, he considered that his was an almost ideal existence. A loving wife, fat children, plenty to eat, good horses, and loyal followers. There was little now to remind Heads Off, chief of the Elk-dog band of the People, that he had once been a young Spanish officer named Juan Garcia.

13
>> >> >>

Cabeza lay in his blankets, a little apart from the others. He was concerned about the manner in which this meeting with the Head Splitters was proceeding.

These people were exceedingly friendly. Many gifts had been exchanged, much feasting had taken place. Their hosts were professing friendship forever and Lizard had become tired from translating endless complimentary speeches.

Cabeza had needed time to think and had retired from the group at the council fire. He was concerned that there had been very little said about the hair-face they sought. Direct questions brought only vague reassurances and reaffirmations of the promise to help.

He could not forget that, according to the Growers, these Head Splitters were the tribe who had most cause to hate the hair-face. Rumor suggested that he might be in this general area. Why, then, did their hosts seem to avoid the subject?

He had approached Sanchez with the question, only to have it shrugged off.

"What do we care of their local politics? Relax, Cabeza! Look how toothsome some of these wenches are!" Sanchez leered at a couple of dark-eyed maidens who happened to pass.

The lieutenant was not satisfied, but did not know where else to turn. Don Pedro was so starry-eyed at the prospects ahead that he would ignore all reason. Cabeza took the precaution of a quiet warning to each of his lancers to remain on the alert and then excused himself to his bed.

Sleep would not come. He tossed and turned, hearing the sounds of the dance drums and the singing from near the council fire. He was painfully aware that no plans had been made for departure or travel on the following day.

He heard a sound and turned his head quickly to see two figures approaching softly. In the moonlight, he saw that one was a native warrior. The other appeared to be a woman. The man shoved her roughly forward, turned abruptly, and walked away.

The girl regained her composure, came a step closer, and stood stiffly, almost at attention. Cabeza rose to an elbow, watched her a moment. She did not move. He raised a hand in question, the all-inclusive query in sign talk.

"What?"

The slender girl seemed surprised for a moment to be addressed in the sign language by a foreigner. Then she quickly rallied and answered in a flurry of hand signs.

"I have been given to you for the night. In the morning, I return to Lean Bull."

Cabeza's first thought was, what fantastic luck! He had seen the girl near the fire and had marveled at her grace and beauty. He tried to tell himself that it was only because he had been on the prairie so long. Finally, as she had walked past in the combined flickering glow of the fire with silvery moonlight, he had had to admit the truth. This was one of the most beautiful women he had ever seen. She carried herself like royalty.

She was tall and straight, her shapely form filling the buckskin dress to perfection. Slim ankles rose to shapely calves which disappeared in the buckskin fringe of her skirt at knee level.

He realized that he was staring. He sat up and motioned her to him. Perhaps, he thought, he should make an effort at conversation.

"Is this the custom of your people?" he signed.

To his amazement, she drew herself up proudly, almost defiantly. The large dark eyes flashed fire.

"These are not my people! I am a prisoner! My people know how to treat women."

She came to him and sat, but there was still the haughty pride, the unyielding defiance that reminded him of the look in the eye of a captured falcon. Caught, imprisoned, it said, but not defeated.

Cabeza began to feel twinges of remorse. He had no aversion to a bed partner. A moment ago, he would have been ready for a quick romp in the blankets, a release of tension, and a good night's sleep. After all, he would never see her again.

Now the situation was different. He had never taken a woman against her will. How could he now, knowing that this was a prisoner? Especially a prisoner who seemed every beautiful inch a princess?

Damn, he told himself. I've spoiled it. Why did I try to make talk? Above all, he was now suddenly feeling concern for the welfare of this girl. As if he did not have enough worries already! Mentally, he kicked himself again and turned to the girl with resignation. Maybe he could get some information through the sign talk.

"How are you called?"

"I am South Wind." She looked puzzled and still defiant. "Why?"

Her signed question made no specific query and Cabeza took it for one about himself. He pointed to his chest.

"Ramon."

There was no way to put his name into sign talk. The girl was still puzzled. Cabeza had not touched her yet, though they sat side by side. She gestured again.

"I do not understand. Do you not want me?"

He smiled and shook his head.

"Not this way. It is not good unless you want, also."

The girl threw back her head and laughed out loud, lovely lilting laughter like water over white pebbles.

"I thought you would be cruel!"

Cabeza glared ferociously at her and both laughed.

"Tell me of your people," he signed.

"We call ourselves 'the People.' Some call us Elk-dog People since we got the elk-dogs. These," she motioned in contempt, "are our enemies. They steal our children, sometimes our women. Ours are prettier than theirs."

Cabeza could well believe this latter statement. It was not a boast, merely a fact, and before him was the proof.

"How did you come here?"

"I was stupid. I went too far from the camp, picking berries. A Head Splitter caught me. I will escape someday."

From what he already knew of this remarkable young woman, he was certain that the Head Splitters could count on it.

"Tell me, South Wind. Do the Head Splitters tell my people truth about the hair-face?"

She snorted in contempt.

"Head Splitters tell no one truth!"

"But, what do they want?"

"Who knows what Head Splitters want? They do not even trust themselves!"

She became confidential.

"I will try to find out if I can!"

"But is there a hair-face?"

"Of course! He is my chief!"

This astonishing bit of information left Cabeza gaping, openmouthed. The girl smiled, then continued.

"He looks like you!" She pointed to his fringe of

beard. "He came to us, five, maybe six summers gone, when I was small. He brought us the elk-dog!"

"How is he called?"

"Heads Off."

Now came the first major communications problem. Cabeza could not understand the signs and the name in the girl's tongue meant nothing to him. Finally, he gave up. There was no way he could think of to determine whether this hair-faced chief was the son of Don Pedro.

The breeze was becoming chilly and the girl shivered a little. He drew the blanket around her shoulders and she leaned against him. The warmth of her body was good, but he was distracted by the information she had given him.

Why, if the Head Splitters knew all about the hair-faced chief, were they not telling the visitors? There was only one answer. For some devious purpose of their own, they preferred to keep the Garcia party uninformed. They must be alert for treachery.

"You will tell me what you can learn? They will do nothing tonight?" She nodded reassuringly and wriggled further into the blankets.

"Rah-mone?" She spoke his name aloud, startling him and attracting his attention. Now they had become conspirators, fellow prisoners, almost.

"Rah-mone," she repeated, continuing her sentence in the sign talk. "I think now it would be good!"

When Ramon Cabeza awoke next morning, the girl was gone.

14
>> >> >>

South Wind bent her head at her work of scraping the buffalo skin. She wished not to attract attention this morning. She had already made a grave mistake in looking too happy.

It infuriated her captor, Lean Bull, to think that she was happy, as she had learned quite early. She made it a point to frequently push him almost to the point of violence by singing at her work. Lean Bull, in retaliation, had tried in all ways to demean her. She had recognized this as his motive last night. He knew full well that, among the People, such use of women was not the custom. He had given her away for the night for the use of a brutal stranger. This would shame her, demean her, and help to break her spirit.

Imagine her own surprise to find a kind and gentle man who was sympathetic to her plight. She had made a grievous mistake, though, when she returned to Lean Bull's lodge in the morning looking radiantly alive and happy.

Lean Bull was furious. He had beaten her and then

assigned her to the attentions of his wives. Of course
they set her at the most disagreeable of their chores
this morning, that of scraping hides.

It would ordinarily have been possible for South
Wind to appear cheerful, even at this task. She had
grown up doing such chores and they presented no
problem to her. She had sometimes purposely continued a cheerful attitude, merely to further irritate Lean
Bull.

But not this morning. Today, she wished to be invisible. She must not attract attention to herself, so
that she might learn more with which to help the
Hairfaces. *Her* hair-face, she thought to herself, trying
hard not to let the joyous tension show.

She had assumed from the first that some form of
treachery was in the offing. Until now, she simply did
not care. What concern of hers that her captors might
kill this party of strange outsiders?

Now they were no longer outsiders, in her mind.
They were of the far distant tribe of her own chief.
This alone could be cause enough to protect them.
But she also had a more personal motive. She must at
all costs help the young subchief, Rah-mone, who
appeared to be the leader of the hair-faced warriors. At
least, they all spoke to him with respect. It was pleas-
ing to her to note that a man such as this, with
leadership abilities, could still be gentle and consider-
ate. This he had proved last night.

South Wind wished so hard to help with his problems that she almost hurt for him. However, no bit of
information came her way. Finally, finished with the
skins, she went to gather firewood. She took a circu-
itous route through the camp, but heard no new information. She began to panic a little. What if the men of
the camp attacked the visitors before she was able to
learn of the plan?

South Wind returned to her captor's lodge and realized that he had visitors. They were inside the lodge,
which in itself was unusual for so hot a day, and were
engaged in animated conversation.

The girl moved close to the side of the lodge cover

and busied herself with arranging her armful of fuel on the ground. She could hear the men plainly and none of the women made any effort to prevent her overhearing. She had gone to great pains not to let her captors know how much of their language she actually understood. If they thought she did not understand, they would ignore her. So she busied herself, assumed a blank expression, and hung on every word.

"They give many gifts," a man was saying.

"Yes, but they have many more. If they stay with us longer, they will give us more."

"They have fine horses, too," Lean Bull spoke. "If we pretend to help them, they will be off-guard. We can kill them at their first night camp and take all the horses and the gifts also. The Elk-dog people are easily two sleeps away."

There was a murmur of approval. South Wind listened further, long enough to determine that this would be the plan. Her captors had determined the general area where the travelers would camp after one day's journey north. They could be attacked while they slept, with very little risk to the attackers. The plotters finally dispersed, though not before the listening girl had departed. She must be sure no one suspected that she had overheard.

Three times that day, she wandered close to the travelers' camp. Each time, she was prevented from contacting Cabeza by the approach of some of the other women. She did not wish to draw attention by making an issue of it, so she temporarily diverted her mission each time.

After darkness fell, South Wind knew that she must make her move. The beat of the dance drums was still throbbing at the council area and there was still feasting and revelry, but not so much as last night. The village was quieting for an earlier sleep tonight.

The girl slipped quietly away and threaded her way among the dark lodges. She was certain she would be followed, but she did not need much time. It would take only a moment to give the warning, once she found Rah-mone. Then they could do with her as they wished. She would have saved the travelers.

It was some time before she found him, walking toward his sleeping robes.

"Rah-mone!" She called softly.

The young man turned, smiling broadly, and held out his arms.

"No!" She shook her head. It was important that she not be distracted. She began to hand sign rapidly.

"You are in great danger!"

"How?"

"They plan to kill you for your horses and supplies. When do you leave?"

"In the morning. When will they try to kill us?"

She was pleased that he was quick and to the point. There was so little time.

"While you sleep, at the first camp. You must be well prepared!"

"Come with us!"

For a few heartbeats, that suggestion appeared the most desirable thing in the world. Then reason returned. It would be too risky to attract the sort of attention that would ensue.

"No." She shook her head firmly. Then, almost by chance, the girl saw, over the shoulder of the young man, an approaching figure. She recognized Lean Bull. Thinking quickly, she threw herself into the arms of the startled Cabeza, embracing him passionately. He instinctively returned the embrace, only to be startled again by the roar of Lean Bull.

"What are you doing here?"

South Wind cowered before him. Good, she thought. He is too angry at my being here to wonder what else might have happened.

"You gave me to him!" she gestured, sobbing.

"Not now! Daughter of a snake! You belong to me!" He gave her a shove. "Go to the lodge!"

His tirade was in his own tongue, but South Wind understood. Even Cabeza grasped the general meaning of the outburst.

"Wait!" he signed. "Let me buy her from you!"

This appeared to further infuriate Lean Bull. He struck out at the girl, the backhand slap knocking her to the ground. Her tormentor whirled to face Cabeza. A knife had appeared in his hand. The other, instantly on guard, drew his belt knife and the two circled warily in the bright moonlight.

Others came running.

"No, Lean Bull!" a man cried out. "He is a guest in our village!"

The newcomer placed himself between the combatants, facing Lean Bull.

"Don't be stupid!" he continued softly. "You will spoil everything. You can kill him tomorrow!"

Slowly, Lean Bull's anger began to cool. He straightened, turned, and walked haughtily away, followed by his friend.

"Come," said the other, "let us eat some more!"

The two walked toward the council fire. Cabeza sheathed his knife and began to breathe more easily. He glanced around, but the girl was gone.

South Wind had slipped quietly away as soon as it became certain there would be no bloodshed. She saw the other man lead Lean Bull away toward the fire and a sudden possibility occurred to her. She hurried to the lodge, went around behind, and approached the horse tied there.

Lean Bull, like most men, kept a horse at his lodge, in case of emergencies. His other horses would be pastured with the main herd, but in this way one animal was always in readiness. It was usually one of Lean Bull's best, but tonight she had noticed that the horse behind the lodge was very special. It was his favorite buffalo runner, a massive spotted stallion. More importantly for her purposes, it was a horse that had never been beaten in a race. If she could get even a short head start, she could not be overtaken.

The horse spoke softly as she untied and led him a few steps away. Swiftly, she used the tether to knot a circle of rawhide around the lower jaw. Every child of the People learned to do this. It was strong medicine, copied after the shiny metal elk-dog medicine brought by Heads Off to the People. Its circle gave control of elk-dogs to the user.

"Where are you going?" the sharp question cut through the shadows.

The girl had been ready to swing up and, for an instant, thought of doing just that. She could ride down the woman in the shadows and keep running. But a better way suggested itself. This was Elk Woman, one of Lean Bull's older wives. She had been kinder than some to the captive and the girl hated to hurt her.

South Wind led the horse toward the figure by the lodge. She carefully turned her face so that the moon illuminated more clearly the puffy welts along her cheek and the swelling of the eye. She sobbed a little.

"Lean Bull hit me, mother! I forgot to water his horse."

Before the woman had time to sort out fact from falsehood, the girl had to act. Boldly, she brushed past, leading the animal toward the stream. Hopefully, it would take the slow-thinking woman a little time to realize that watering Lean Bull's horse was not one of the captive's duties.

Out of sight of the lodge, South Wind swung gracefully to the horse's back and held him at a walk until they reached the stream.

She let him drink only a little, then walked him quietly up the bank on the far side. The stallion was eager to run, but she held him in until they passed the crest of the hill. Then she put heels to his ribs and settled into a steady lope, guiding her direction by the Real-star in the north.

Now, if she could only reach her people in time to bring help.

15
»   »   »

South Wind let the horse have his head as they wound their way up a long slope to the crest of the ridge. It was almost full daylight. In a few moments, Sun Boy would thrust his torch over the rim of the earth and day would begin.

This would be a good time to stop and let the horse rest and graze. Through the night, there had been no sound of pursuit, but that meant little. Most important was the question of how long it had taken Elk Woman to realize what had happened. When had the woman become certain that the girl was not coming back with the horse? And after that, how long until she mustered enough courage to give the alarm?

South Wind had taken another precaution. Her initial direction of travel had been due north. Then, when opportunity offered, she had walked the horse across a gravelly bend of a stream. They followed the stream's course for a while, stepping in the water to leave no tracks. Another rocky riffle gave opportunity to leave the watercourse and the girl directed their course more northeasterly. She had a fair idea of the general area where the People would be camped. If she could only find them!

The horse stepped the last few paces and emerged on the flat, level hilltop. South Wind took a quick look around and saw nothing alarming. She swung down stiffly, walked a few steps, and then stood, letting the horse graze while she watched the back trail.

She could see for a long distance in the crisp morning air. The rolling prairie, smooth and light green in color, was dotted with scattered bands of buffalo, elk, and antelope. The courses of several small streams were marked by slashes of darker green. Soft plumes of mist arose along the watercourses. The prairie was coming awake. Birds sang a spectacular morning song in honor of Sun Boy.

The total picture was one of such peace and security that the tired girl was lulled into complacence. She did not even hear the warrior emerge from a fringe of sumac behind her. Her first inkling of trouble was a surprised snort from the stallion. Before she had time to turn, there was a sudden rush and she was pinioned from behind.

South Wind had not come this far to be caught so easily. She had no weapon, but this would not prevent a fight. In a sudden flurry, she loosed a series of blows. A jab in the ribs with an elbow, a kick here, a blow there, a knee in the groin. The two rolled on the ground, the girl continuing to claw, bite, and jab. She loosed a stream of invectives at her opponent, including some very uncomplimentary remarks about his maternal ancestry.

Suddenly, his grasp relaxed and, in a moment, the man was laughing.

"Stop! Stop!" The plea was in her own language. "South Wind? Is it you?"

Dumbfounded, the girl stopped her struggle long enough to take a good look at her assailant.

"Long Elk! What are you doing here?"

How fortunate, she was thinking. Long Elk, one of

the respected Elk-dog Society, a son of Coyote, was a brother-in-law of Chief Heads Off. Without waiting for an answer, she hurried on.

"We must hurry and bring the warriors. The Head Splitters are ready to kill the people from the tribe of Heads Off."

Long Elk was still rubbing his bruised anatomy. Blood oozed slowly from a deep scratch on his cheek.

"I know. *Aiee*, you have sharp knees and elbows. How did they ever catch you?"

"Long Elk, listen to me. There are Hairfaces in the Head Splitter camp. They look for Heads Off. I think the old man is our chief's father."

"We know, little one. That is why I am here. We watch. We do not wish our chief to go back to his tribe."

"But what does Heads Off say?"

"He does not know. We are afraid he will leave us."

The girl was furious. "You have not even told him that his people are here? Then how can we go and help them?"

Long Elk shrugged. "It is no concern of ours. Let the Head Splitters kill the Hairfaces. Then there is no problem."

He thought for a moment that the girl would attack him again.

"You would let the enemy kill our chief's father and never tell him? You are a society of cowards, not warriors!"

"Perhaps we could talk to Coyote and White Buffalo. But first, we must attend to that." He pointed far across the prairie, where a file of warriors were crawling over the crest of a distant ridge like so many ants. "Get your horse."

The girl was quickly on the horse and Long Elk returned with his own mount, previously hidden in the sumac brush. He unwound the thong from the animal's nose, which had prevented its calling out to the other horse.

"Did you steal the best horse they had?" he asked admiringly.

"I hope so! Which way?"

Long Elk led the way across the flat top of the hill and into the broken rock on the other slope.

"We will use the buffalo to cover our tracks." He pointed to a distant herd.

The girl nodded and fell in beside him as they reached better footing.

"Long Elk," she insisted again. "They plan to kill them at the night camp—tonight!"

The warrior nodded. "I see. We will talk to Coyote. Now we must go."

The two had threaded their way half through the scattered herd before their pursuers topped the rise. The great shaggy beasts moved lazily aside or merely raised massive heads to stare. They continued their deliberate course, knowing that sudden movement might urge the animals into a running frenzy.

The distance was so great that it was questionable whether the pursuers ever actually saw them. The riders bent low and mingled with the buffalo. When they at least reached the far side of the herd, Long Elk untied his robe from behind him on his saddle pad. He selected a yearling bull and rode straight toward it at a charge, flapping the robe wildly. The startled animal whirled, crashed into a grazing cow, and the two galloped wildly into the herd. Other animals began to run and, in the space of a few heartbeats, the entire herd was shaking the earth with the thunder of a thousand hooves.

Long Elk led the way to a low hillock for better visibility. They could look back over their recent path for any pursuit. Through the thin mist of dust rising from the buffalo herd, they could see the tiny specks of the distant riders. The herd was now heading precisely in their direction. For a few moments, the Head Splitters milled uncertainly, then turned to retreat.

The two young People sat on their horses and watched, as the entire enemy party broke and ran before the onslaught of the herd. Their last glimpse before the cloud of rising dust obscured their vision was that of scurrying warriors retreating up the slope

Long Elk leaned back and wiped tears of laughter from his eyes. *"Aiee,"* he chortled, "it was better than I planned!"

South Wind agreed, but was impatient to be on the way. She kneed her horse forward.

"In a moment, little one," he called to her.

He looked around the earth's rim, glanced at Sun Boy, and then pointed to a clump of trees on the horizon.

"That way," he said. "Now we ride!"

He struck out at a long lope and South Wind was hard put to match his pace.

16

The two riders made excellent time. Both were well mounted and Long Elk knew the route exactly so there was little delay.

At the first rest stop, they chewed dried pemmican from Long Elk's pouch while the horses grazed hungrily. The warrior examined both animals carefully. Much depended on their condition. Both appeared in top shape, ready for the all-important mission.

Long Elk suggested, however, that they exchange mounts. He was a big man and the stamina of Lean Bull's buffalo runner, best of the enemy's herds, might be needed before the night was over. His own horse, slightly smaller, could still easily carry the girl's lighter weight.

Regretfully, South Wind gave up the stallion. She had never ridden so fine an animal. She realized, however, that Long Elk's logic was correct.

"Remember," she admonished, "he is still mine! I stole him!"

Long Elk laughed and nodded, swinging up in one lithe motion to continue travel.

By pushing to the limit of the animals' endurance, they were able to continue travel through the night. It was nearing dawn when Long Elk pointed ahead. Almost at the same moment, the girl's nostrils caught a stray puff of night breeze which carried the unmistakable odor of the village ahead.

South Wind would have ridden in, shouting to raise the sleeping People, but Long Elk was very firm.

"No! You must wait here with the horses! I will go and bring the medicine man."

The girl looked for a moment as if she would break and run for the camp, but Long Elk saw her intent.

"South Wind, it is very important." He spoke gently but firmly. "You must stay here in the trees. I will tie you if I must, but I would rather not. I will return as soon as I can. Give me your word that you will stay here!"

Reluctantly, she nodded.

It seemed a long time before she heard him returning, bringing two others. In the gray of dawn, she recognized White Buffalo and Coyote, the latter sleepily rubbing his eyes.

"Now, little one, tell them what you have told me."

South Wind quickly sketched in her story, skipping part of the description of her own emotional involvement. The older men listened attentively, punctuating her narrative with an occasional exclamation of surprise.

"So," asked Coyote as she finished and paused for breath, "you think the old hair-face is the father of our chief?"

The girl nodded vehemently.

"Why do you think so?" White Buffalo spoke probingly. "How could you tell? It is said that the Hairfaces all look alike!"

"That is true, uncle. Still, he carries himself much like Heads Off and sits well on his elk-dog."

The men shook their heads in indecision. South Wind's temper began to flare.

"You would sit here and wonder such things while our enemy may be killing the people of our chief's tribe?"

Her voice was becoming high and shrill with emotion. Still, it had apparently not occurred to the others how deep a personal involvement the girl might have.

"The Head Splitters were to attack them last night. I was able to warn them." She was very close to tears.

"Then," observed Long Elk in a practical tone, "our problem may be already over!"

"True," shrugged White Buffalo. "It is no matter, either way."

Coyote had been thinking deeply.

"My friends," he mused at last, "I think we have made a mistake."

He turned to the old medicine man.

"Uncle, when you and I asked Heads Off to lead the People, we promised to help him, because he did not know our ways. Now, I think we have not helped him in this. We were so afraid of losing our chief that we have done him wrong."

The others sat, silent, knowing that he spoke truth.

"How can a chief lead," he continued, "if his people conceal from him as we have done? This matter needs the decision of a chief. It is not for us to decide."

It was a long and serious speech for the usually quick and jovial Coyote. Everyone was still for a moment and finally White Buffalo spoke sadly, to no one in particular.

"Coyote is right."

"Then what is to be done?" Long Elk asked.

Coyote heaved a deep sigh.

"Someone must tell him."

South Wind was by now completely frustrated at the course of the discussion.

"*I* will tell him!" she almost shouted at them, turning to her horse.

"Wait, little one," Coyote spoke sadly. "We will all go."

The strangely assorted little group was seen by only a few early risers as they threaded their way among the lodges. Heads Off was just emerging sleepily from his lodge when they arrived there. He rapidly came fully awake at the seriousness of their approach.

"*Ah-koh,*" he greeted, waiting for someone to speak.

"Tell him, daughter." It was White Buffalo who opened the exchange.

Rapidly, South Wind told her story. The chief listened intently, nodding occasionally. When she reached the point of her encounter with Long Elk, he stopped her, furiously turning on the young warrior.

"You *knew* of this? Why was I not told?"

"My chief," White Buffalo intervened, "we were afraid that if people of your own tribe came, you would go away with them."

Heads Off looked quickly from one to the other.

"You *all* knew? And I was not told?" The accusatory question was thrust directly at Coyote.

Coyote nodded.

"It is as White Buffalo said."

"You did not trust me to do what is best for the People?"

No one answered and, for a long moment, they were left to wonder how Heads Off would react next. At their hurt and dejected expressions, however, the young chief's mood seemed to soften.

"No matter now." He turned to Long Elk. "Spread the word. A council, as soon as we can gather."

Heads Off turned on his heel and strode purposefully toward the council ring.

17
» » »

A council in the early morning was an almost unheard of thing among the People. Word spread rapidly and people hurried to assemble. It had to be a matter of extreme importance to initiate such a council. There was hardly anyone who stayed away, though at most councils many were too bored to attend.

The council opened quickly. South Wind was the heroine of the hour, having just escaped several moons of captivity by the enemy. Her story was improving with retelling and she made a dramatic presentation, ending with a plea to help the Hairfaces. Many hearts were moved.

"There are many here who knew of these Hairfaces."

Heads Off glanced around the circle at the members of the Elk-dog Society. Some hung their heads, expecting a reprimand, but the chief continued.

"You have had time to consider the matter. Tell us your thoughts."

Hesitantly at first, then more freely, discussion began to flow around the circle.

Soon three distinct attitudes became apparent. One strong faction was willing to let well enough alone. If the Hairfaces and the enemy Head Splitters destroyed each other, so much the better. That would remove two threats.

Almost at opposites, but with similar motives, were the more militant warriors of the tribe. These were primarily members of the Blood Society. They wished to fight on the side of anyone who would fight Head Splitters, the traditional enemy.

The third faction were those who strongly felt that the Hairfaces should be helped, if only because they were of the tribe of Heads Off. This group grew rapidly in strength, urged on by South Wind. The girl was very persuasive and very vocal. By this time, she felt certain that the old man who led the Hairfaces was the father of Heads Off. And it made little difference, she argued. If he were not the chief's father, he might have been. They should help the Hairfaces, just as they would help one of the other bands of the People in similar circumstances. It was a matter of blood, of common heritage.

Heads Off attempted to stay out of the discussion to form an objective opinion. Someone asked if this *could* be his father and he had to admit that he did not know. It hardly seemed likely, but was not impossible. Even as he said it, the young chief had a strange feeling of detachment, as if he were speaking of someone else. His life as Juan Garcia seemed worlds away. He had become thoroughly one of the People. Yet there was a gnawing doubt, an unresolved question in the back of his mind. Could this actually be his father, come to search for him? Even at the time, his foremost thoughts were of what effect this might have on his adopted people. He thought of his family, his friends in the tribe. How would they be affected by contact with the Spanish, whether it was his father or not?

His attention swung back to the circle, where Coyote was speaking. Heads Off had seen the keen mind of his father-in-law shift and probe at the question, changing his position. It had become obvious that Coyote had been instrumental in the concealment of the developments. It was just as obvious that he had done so for the good of the People and Heads Off found it easy to forgive.

Now it was equally apparent that the new information was swinging Coyote's opinion closer to that of South Wind.

"—and I think," he was saying, "that it makes little difference who these Hairfaces are. If they are enemies of the Head Splitters, they are friends of the People!"

There was a shout of approval from the Blood Society and much shaking of weapons in the air. It appeared that the collective thought of the People was reaching unanimity.

"We must hurry before we are too late!" cried South Wind.

Yet there remained one more thing.

"White Buffalo," called the chief, "can you give us a vision, uncle?"

The old medicine man shuffled forward and spread a tanned skin on the ground. Its inner surface was decorated with painted designs and mystic symbols. Crow Woman beat the ceremonial drum while her husband circled in dance steps around the painted skin.

Apparently, many thought the outcome a foregone conclusion. Men were running here and there, obtaining their weapons and catching up their best horses. In the distance, someone exuberantly voiced the full-throated war cry of the People.

White Buffalo continued to chant and the mind of Heads Off raced ahead. The village must be defended and they could leave that in charge of the Bowstring Society. They were older, proven warriors, most of whom had been initiated before the advent of the horse. They were experts in the art of warfare on foot.

They would do an admirable job of looking after the village.

The war party would include members of both the Elk-dog and the Blood societies. Heads Off was a trifle uneasy. The headstrong Bloods had nearly caused the annihilation of the People only a season ago, but then relented and returned to join in combat against the Head Splitters.

Heads Off caught the eye of Red Dog, leader of the Blood Society, and motioned to him. The warrior approached, standing proud and stiff before his chief, and Heads Off had the ludicrous idea for a moment that the young man was about to salute.

"Red Dog," he asked quietly, "can we count on the Bloods to stay with the war party and act well?"

"My chief," Red Dog's face lit up, "the Bloods are ready to follow you anywhere!"

Heads Off smiled. He well remembered the surprise charge by the rebel Bloods which had saved the day for the People and brought them back together. Red Dog himself had led the assault, routing the enemy. There was no question of the bravery of the Bloods, only of their judgment. That would remain to be seen. However, the chief was inclined to think that the problems of discipline were behind them. Red Dog seemed a sensible subchief, although young.

White Buffalo had reached the end of his chant and dropped to his knees before the painted skin. People came running to watch the end of the ceremony. The medicine man raised his arms and turned his face to the sky for just a few moments more of the chant. It was always good to have a large audience.

Finally, he raised the horn high and, with a magnificent sweeping gesture, cast its contents across the skin. Small bits of wood, horn, bone, and bright pebbles bounced and skittered across the colored surface and came to rest.

There was absolute quiet. The old man squinted and poked at the small objects on the skin, then stiffly rose to go and stand before the chief. Crow Woman began to gather up the equipment of her husband's profession.

"My chief," White Buffalo announced clearly, "the signs are good!"

There was a rising chorus of shouts as warriors rushed for their horses.

18
>> >> >>

Cabeza sat loosely in the saddle as they traveled, his thoughts a confused jumble. He was alert to the possibility of danger, but felt that the time was not now. According to the girl, South Wind, they would be attacked in night camp tonight.

He was inclined to believe her and, in fact, was certain that she could be trusted. After all, the girl had come to warn him, at considerable risk to herself. It had all happened so rapidly, yet there were some things about her evening visit to him that were evident.

Most obvious was the wrath of Lean Bull. Cabeza was puzzled over the man's change in attitude. That first night, he had practically thrown the girl at the visitor, yet he had later appeared almost jealous of their relationship.

And that was another puzzling thing. Even allowing for the great differences in their cultures, Cabeza thought that he was an accurate judge of people. The emotions that the girl had shown reflected something more than the ordinary. Unless he was badly mis-

taken, South Wind was exhibiting genuine affection—
and of a rather special sort. Again, he recalled that she
had risked her life to warn him of the danger ahead.

This line of thought called his mind again to the
odd direction his own feelings had taken. He could
still hardly believe that he had almost been involved
in a fight with knives over a woman. Mother of God,
that was the sort of thing that happened in sordid
taverns and brothels and back alleys. Yet it had happened to him, merely because he had tried to protect
the girl. That had seemed only a gentlemanly thing to
do at the time.

At least, that was what Cabeza kept trying to convince himself. There were other disturbing thoughts.
He was irritated that he was unable to remove the girl
from his mind for very long at a time. He repeatedly
wondered what was to become of her. After the Garcia party had left the area, Cabeza would no longer be
able to protect her. The very thought made him feel
sad and depressed.

Then the young lieutenant would shake his head in
disbelief. He could not be concerned with the welfare
of every young native on the plains. Yet, even as he
derided his own stupidity, he would remind himself
once more that this was no ordinary native girl. South
Wind was a special person who had not only shown
special feeling for him, but had risked her life to warn
him of danger. He kept coming back to that and felt
that his thoughts were moving in a circle.

He glanced over at the well-armed native who rode
a few paces to his left. Cabeza was not certain how
the travelers were expected to regard this native escort. It was clear that Don Pedro Garcia considered
the contingent of warriors a sort of military honor
guard. He seemed pleased and flattered.

True, the native leader had been convincing when
the party of travelers had prepared to depart. Vowing
friendship and assistance, he had announced by means
of the sign talk that warriors would accompany them
to show the way. He himself would go, Lean Bull
announced.

Cabeza suspected other motives. There had been an unpleasant scene shortly after daylight. The native chief had approached the Garcia camp in a rage. He flatly accused Cabeza of stealing his horse and the young woman, South Wind. Only by much persuasion on the part of Lizard and some of his own people could Lean Bull be convinced. His missing property was simply not there.

He then made the accusation that there was some plot for the escaped girl to meet the travelers later with the stolen horse. Again, Cabeza denied the accusation. Privately, the young man wished he *had* been able to formulate such a plan.

Finally, Lean Bull tired of his harangue and turned away, obviously not convinced. Later, he appeared with the "honor guard" as they were about to depart. By this time, he was smiling and full of friendship again, though he avoided Cabeza.

Cabeza was convinced that there were ulterior motives here. First, it was obvious that if the runaway girl did try to contact the Garcia party, she might be recaptured and the horse recovered. Beyond that, as the day wore on, Cabeza became more and more convinced that the warning of South Wind was accurate. The present situation placed a war party of well-armed Head Splitters in or near the camp of the travelers when it became time for the night halt.

So far, Cabeza had spoken to no one of his warning from the girl. It would be necessary, of course, but he could wait for a time. He might discover more information about the plot. Then he could inform the others. Meanwhile, he was as friendly and jovial as he dared, to the warrior on his left, especially.

He tried to engage the other in conversation in the sign talk, but the native was noncommunicative. He answered either very briefly or not at all.

Cabeza's suspicions were strengthened after a noon rest halt. Lean Bull approached Garcia with dignity and announced that they were returning to their village. Two men, he added, somewhat as an afterthought, would stay with the travelers for a time to guide them on the way. Garcia was profuse in his thanks.

How clever, thought Cabeza. They now have spies in our camp. The others stay back just out of sight, ready to attack when the spies give the word. He must speak to Don Pedro.

It was nearing evening before he found opportunity to ride next to the old man and share his information.

"*Señor* Garcia, I must speak with you of serious matters."

"Yes, Ramon, what is it?"

The elder man was so cheerful, so optimistic and exuberant, that Cabeza was almost reluctant to lay the burden he carried on the proud old shoulders. But he had to. He kneed his black horse closer and lowered his tone.

"I have cause, *señor*, to think we may be attacked tonight."

True to his military training, Garcia's facial expression never changed. He sat the gray mare and looked straight ahead as he responded calmly.

"Why do you think so, Lieutenant?"

Rapidly, Cabeza sketched in the events of the past two days, some of which Garcia already knew. The young man skipped lightly over his true feelings for the girl, but Don Pedro was observant. He smiled.

"You like this girl a great deal, Ramon?"

"More important, sir, I trust her!"

Garcia nodded.

"I wondered what the scene this morning was all about. Are you certain about this attack?"

"Oh no, *señor*. But the girl was. And everything fits. Do you not think it strange that our escort left us, but left spies?"

"Guides, Lieutenant," Garcia laughed.

Then he sobered.

"Yes, Ramon, I did think it odd. It will do well to be on guard and no harm is done if we are wrong."

The two men rode in silence for a time, then Garcia spoke again.

"You must quietly alert your lancers and the bowmen, but be sure they do not arouse suspicion. I will do the same with the others. When we camp, put your blanket near mine."

He wheeled the gray horse and sauntered off, as if they had merely been discussing the weather. Cabeza continued for a time in the casual fashion of a bored traveler. Then he reined over to ride beside bushy-bearded Sergeant Perez of the lancers.

In this way, the word spread quietly, with the caution not to take any overt action or even to look as if anything were suspected.

The routine chores of setting up camp proceeded as twilight drew near. Cabeza spread his blankets near those of Don Pedro and joined the old man as he sat on a rock to contemplate the evening.

"Do you notice anything, Ramon?"

"No, sir."

"Nor do I. But we must watch those two."

The sky darkened and the stars began to come out. Cabeza watched as the men, one by one, sought their blankets. Finally, he rose, stretched and yawned, and, bidding a loud good night to Garcia, turned to his bed. The older man soon followed.

The camp was quiet, the fires only piles of warm white ashes, and Cabeza was still wide awake. The Great Bear had swung only a fraction of his nightly circle in the northern sky when one, then the other, of the natives rose quietly to his feet and slipped silently into the darkness.

The lieutenant reached to alert Garcia, but the old man's voice showed that he, too, observed.

"Wait a few moments, Ramon. Then we will wake the others. There is much to do."

19
» » »

Lean Bull lay in the shade of a gigantic old oak tree and waited for time to pass. Not until well after dark would his scouts return to bring word of their quarry. Meanwhile, the war party waited, hidden in a heavily wooded canyon. Some of the warriors gambled, rolling the plum stones on a robe spread skin-side upward. Others slept. Lean Bull was too preoccupied with his thoughts.

Much had happened in the past three suns. First, the hair-faced strangers, seeking a hair-face living among the people of the prairie. From the descriptions, it appeared that the man they sought was Lean Bull's sworn enemy, leader of the Elk-dog people. It had seemed good to pretend to help the travelers, taking their gifts and deluding them with promises of help.

Then there had been the other developments. It had seemed a logical way to punish the unruly slave girl, to give her to one of the strangers.

Sometimes, Lean Bull had wished that he had never

seized her. But it had been so easy. He had been on a scouting expedition and had blundered upon the girl, where she should not have been, and it seemed foolish not to take advantage of the situation. He rode down on her with his horse, scooped the running girl to the back of the animal, and made his retreat. She had fought like a spotted cat and finally he had been forced to knock her half-senseless with the handle of his war club to quiet her.

And that, he recalled, had been only the beginning. Lean Bull had several wives, as was the custom among his people. Still, he took the captive girl to wife, his right by tradition as her captor. Unless, of course, he wanted to sell her. He probably should have done that. Instead, he tried, by every means he could think of, to break the girl's spirit and bring her under his command.

True, she did as she was told, but her attitude never changed. She was proud, defiant, even cheerful. The way she sang at difficult, malodorous tasks became infuriating to Lean Bull. He actually began to worry a little. Sooner or later, he knew she would try to escape. When she did, it was not impossible that she might also try to kill her captor. Such things had happened and this defiant woman would be just the sort to try such a crazy thing.

Then, when the strangers came, Lean Bull thought of an ideal scheme. At least, it seemed so at the time. He knew that among the tribe of the captive girl, women were regarded differently. They were not bought and sold, even captive women. This seemed wasteful to Lean Bull, but he had heard that it went even further. Women of South Wind's tribe, he had heard, could even own property and could speak in the councils.

What an excellent way, he schemed, to teach a woman with such ideas her proper place. He would give her to one of the hairy strangers, to do with as he wished. The young subchief who appeared to be the leader of the hair-faced warriors. When that one was finished with her, he would probably give her to some of his spearmen. By the time they had spent the night with her, the girl should be happy with her lot in the lodge of Lean Bull.

But something had gone wrong. Apparently, the young chief had kept her for himself all night and the two had become friends. That the pretty young captive would prefer the company of a hair-faced stranger to his own became intolerable to Lean Bull. His scheme had turned sour and was replaced by the bitterness of jealousy.

His hatred focused on Cabeza and, especially after the incident with the knife, Lean Bull had decided. That one must die and he would take great delight in carrying out the act.

Yet, even before he was able to accomplish this, another insult was heaped upon Lean Bull. The girl had disappeared and, with her, his best buffalo horse. Slow-witted old Elk Woman had actually seen the girl go and had said nothing till morning. She professed to think that the captive was only watering the stallion.

Lean Bull was certain that the hair-faced young chief was involved, but could not prove it. No matter. When darkness came, he would have the pleasure of cutting that one's throat. He fully expected to find the escaped captive in the travelers' camp also. Maybe he would cut her throat, too. It seemed a waste, but she had been such a problem so far.

Yes, that was probably best. He would have his vengeance and would claim not only his own horse, but the black stallion of the hair-face. Let the others divide the supplies and goods the strangers carried.

So intent was Lean Bull on his revenge, that he decided to forego one of the basic taboos of his people. It was widely believed among the Head Splitters that a person dying during the night risks losing his soul. The disembodied spirit, lost in the darkness, may wander forever. For this reason, they would rarely engage in battle during the hours of darkness.

Lean Bull, confident in his ruse to surprise the stranger, had planned his attack at night. The travelers, he assured his followers, would be as helpless as an orphan buffalo calf before wolves. There would be no risk at all. They could creep among the sleeping men and, at a signal, wield the massive stone war clubs that were the mark of their tribe.

Except, Lean Bull brooded, he wished to use the knife. It would be so gratifying if the hated hair-face were able to know, for a moment before he died, who his assailant was. Then Lean Bull could use his war club on the girl and the others as opportunity presented.

Darkness finally descended and Lean Bull rolled in his buffalo robe to sleep a bit while waiting for the scouts. It seemed forever and he slept little. He had just dozed off when there was a stirring in the camp. He tossed aside his robe and reached for his weapons.

"They are camped where we expected?"

"Yes, my chief," the scout nodded. "I can show you where the young hair-faced leader sleeps."

It was good.

"What of the girl?"

The scout spread his palms in perplexity.

"The girl is not with them."

20

» » »

Lean Bull crawled forward, one of the scouts at his elbow. Peering through the fringe of brush, he could see a clearing in the dim starlight. Recumbent figures lay scattered about the area and dying fires smoldered without giving light.

The scout pointed ahead, indicating two figures close together on the west side of the encampment.

"The old chief and the young war chief," he whispered.

Lean Bull nodded.

"The young chief is mine. His black horse, also."

The black stallion and a gray mare grazed on picket lines nearby.

"Yes, my chief."

He pointed beyond the camp.

"There are thin woods to the north. Those we do not kill will run there and we can hunt them in the morning."

"It is good."

The two squirmed backward and made their way back to the rest of the party, waiting beyond the next range of hills. A small fire burned low. Lean Bull squatted and beckoned his warriors.

By the light of the fire, he sketched a rude map showing the scattered slopes, the fires, and the semicircle of woods on the north.

"We will crawl up close. I will cut the throat of the young war chief first, so they are without a leader. Then, when I give the war cry, we will all strike the others. We can divide their supplies and horses in the morning."

Quietly, the group moved out, following single file the route indicated by the scouts. There was still plenty of darkness left when they arrived in the vicinity of the travelers' camp. In silence, the warriors spread in an attack line and began to crawl forward toward their assault positions.

When everyone seemed ready, Lean Bull snaked forward, wriggling flat on his belly, raising his head ever so slightly to keep proper direction. A horse stomped and nickered softly and he dropped flat for a long moment to see if any activity ensued. There was none.

The crawler neared his quarry and paused to look around for a sentry. He saw none and reflected for a moment on the stupidity of the strangers.

Now he could see the long form of the sleeper before him. The sleeping robe was drawn up around the ears and it appeared that the man's back was toward him. Lean Bull slipped the razor-sharp flint knife from his waist and took it firmly in his right hand. It would be a simple matter now to slide close enough to throw back the robe, grasp the hair with his left hand, and make one swift slash across the throat with the blade.

He flipped the blanket aside and the grasping left hand encountered no hair, but a smooth, hard surface. What he had taken for the head of the sleeper rolled away, a smooth, round stone. His sequence of motion already begun, the knife was already thrusting downward, but slashed across emptiness. It glanced off the rotted end of the log which stimulated a sleeping body.

Confused, unwilling to admit that he had been duped, Lean Bull voiced the yipping war cry of his tribe and the others rushed forward. Now several of the recumbent figures showed signs of life. A heavy multiple twang could be plainly heard as the Spanish crossbowmen released a volley. Shooting from the prone position, they had their unsuspecting targets silhouetted against the night sky. The short, heavy crossbow bolts found their marks with deadly accuracy. At least four Head Splitters would, this very night, have the opportunity to test the tradition of souls wandering in darkness.

The others pressed forward, swinging clubs at the bundled robes. There were exclamations of astonishment as the weapons struck logs, stones, and brush.

At that moment, there was a shout and a rush from the fringe of the scrubby trees. Cabeza led the charge, with a lance at the ready before him. At his side was Don Pedro himself, exuberantly wielding his great sword and roaring with the joy of joining battle once more. Close behind came the lancers, fighting on foot, closing in from the wings of the half circle of trees. Scattered among the professional soldiers were the Garcia servants, armed with an odd assortment of short swords, knives, even sticks, clubs, and stones.

The entire effect was too much for the surprised Head Splitters. The warriors broke and ran, followed by another volley of crossbow bolts. Only one or two of the lancers were even able to overtake a fleeing adversary.

Cabeza called them back from pursuit. It would make little sense to run into the darkness after armed warriors.

Now Lean Bull called together the angry remnants of his war party. There was much shouting and accusation. Everyone had lost friends in the attack and their leader's credibility was badly damaged.

"Our chief has gone mad over that cursed girl!" someone accused.

"We should never have attacked at night!"

Lean Bull held up a hand for attention.

"Listen, my friends! We did not know that these strangers like to fight in the dark. Now we do, so we will avoid it. We will attack them after daylight. They are few and many of them are not even warriors. We must avenge our fallen friends."

In the end, the possibility of revenge became the overpowering emotion. Lean Bull was not without his powers of persuasion and he was known as a leader in battle. Soon enthusiasm for the kill returned. The entire party took the back trail to retrieve their horses. Only Lean Bull and one scout remained to observe and plan.

Dawn was breaking by the time the others returned, leading the horses of the fallen, as well as those of Lean Bull and the scout. The interval had allowed time for the warriors to work themselves into a frenzy of excitement.

"We must be cautious," Lean Bull warned. "Let us wait until they are spread out on the trail. Then we can strike and scatter them."

He took his horse from the man who led it and moved to an area near the top of the slope. Here they could relax and observe the travelers as they prepared to move out.

21

>> >> >>

Don Pedro was exuberant as the sun rose that morning. His party had repulsed the attack without loss of life. The only casualties were two. A lancer's left eye and cheek were grossly swollen from a glancing blow with a war club and one of the servants limped painfully. He had run into a jagged rock in the dark.

The old don worried not at all at the treachery they had experienced. That was only to be expected. Such were the ways of diplomacy. He could remember well a campaign in northern Italy, many years ago. During the course of things, they had spent a delightful evening drinking and carousing with the dragoons of a local governor's military unit. Next day, they had been attacked by the same troops. No matter. There were no hard feelings. Each was only doing his job.

And it was only the same with these savages, Don Pedro thought. He had tried bribery and failed. No, not completely. They had had a pleasant interlude, secured provisions, and had learned of the hair-faced chief of some other tribe. That might be valuable information.

True, the facts were sketchy. Young Cabeza was inclined to attribute that to the fact that the hair-face was considered an enemy by the Head Splitters. He was probably correct. In addition, that fact did nothing to enhance any ties of friendship between that tribe and the travelers.

Then there was the matter of the girl. It was too bad she had disappeared. She might have given much valuable information. The young lieutenant, however, had spent many hours with her. Undoubtedly pleasant hours, Garcia chuckled to himself. More importantly, he had learned much from the girl about the hair-faced chief of her people. The old man was impressed that the basic facts were correct—in time, place, and circumstance.

He longed to question the girl himself. Perhaps she would return or maybe they would encounter some of her people. At any rate, their course seemed clear. They must move in a northerly direction and let come what might.

A more pressing problem was that of the Head Splitters. The little group of travelers had successfully met a surprise attack. They had killed four and, from the bloodstains discovered in the camp after daylight, at least three more had been severely wounded, to crawl away in the darkness.

Some of the party were certain that the savages had been taught a lesson. They would not return after so disastrous a rout. Don Pedro, the old campaigner, disagreed. Unless he judged his man very wrongly, he thought the one called Lean Bull would never give up. And, of course, Don Pedro's profession was the judging of men and their tenacity.

Evaluating last night's surprise raid, Don Pedro thought it merely an error of judgment on Lean Bull's part. The thing had looked too easy and the man had simply underestimated his adversary. An easy mistake. One he might have made himself in younger days, he reflected.

Now, the question was, what would the savages do next? As Don Pedro saw it, there were two possibilities. Another attack was certain, the only question being when it would come.

The party which had accompanied them as an escort the previous day had been only about the size of their own. It was now somewhat smaller, with the loss of at least four men. Furthermore, their intended victims were now forewarned of the danger.

The prudent thing for Lean Bull to do would be to send back for more warriors. They would be needed for an all-out assault. Of course, it would take nearly two days for the reinforcements to return to this point and the travelers would be moving in the meantime, forcing rapid pursuit.

This brought the other possibility to mind, that Lean Bull would strike immediately. There were advantages to this plan. He could send for reinforcements, but meanwhile attack and harass the travelers. This would delay their progress until the other warriors arrived.

Either way, it seemed likely that there would be some sort of attack before the day was out.

Don Pedro threw the saddle on the gray mare and tightened the girth. He had always insisted on saddling his own horse. No one else could quite do it properly.

He glanced around the camp. There was a general feeling of optimism at the success of the defense. That was good, but not too much so. They must be cautioned.

Ramon Cabeza approached, leading his black horse. "*Señor* Garcia, I would speak with you. I think we will be attacked today."

It is good, thought Don Pedro. This young man, son of my friend, will make a great leader. He has already anticipated the enemy's moves. I will not have to explain it to him.

"Yes, Lieutenant, what do you plan?"

"I think, *señor*, we should push north as rapidly as

possible. We may be able to keep ahead of any reinforcements they send for."

Garcia nodded noncommittally and was inwardly
pleased. Ramon was planning well. He was equally
pleased to note that there was no question of changing
direction or turning back. The major quest of the
expedition was not even questioned. It would go
forward.

Cabeza spoke briefly to the group prior to departure.
He warned of impending attack and redistributed his
forces. Lancers would ride four abreast, two squads
before and two behind, instead of the usual double
file. This would shorten the column and make it less
vulnerable to scattering if they were struck.

Likewise, those on foot were placed in the middle of
the column of march for their protection. If attack
came, the lancers would circle to form a perimeter
with the baggage and foot servants in the center, along
with the crossbowmen. The plan was a good one, Don
Pedro thought. He could have done no better himself.

The bowmen were not happy with this new arrangement. They had been leading the column directly behind the three officers of the party. It was bad
enough to follow three horses, they grumbled. Now
they were behind two whole squads of mounted lancers. Such an indignity was unworthy of weapons spe-
cialists such as they. Still, the grumbling was minimal
and allegiance to Cabeza was strong. Had the lieutenant not executed the successful defense last night?

Everyone was urged to drink well and to fill all
available waterskins at the cold spring beside the camp.
The horses were watered and the command to mount
rang out.

They would travel as rapidly as the pace of those on
foot would allow. There would be only brief rest stops
and, at least for today, there would be no noon halt.

22

>> >> >>

Twice that morning, the Head Splitters made a feinting attack, but stopped outside of weapon range. Even the crossbowmen, with their long-range projectiles, refrained from launching them.

The net result was only that the party was delayed each time while the lancers formed a defense perimeter. After the second encounter, Cabeza recognized the maneuver for what it was—a delaying tactic. The word was passed to keep moving, but merely to protect the flank from which the attack came. Then, if the enemy wished to cause delay, he would have to force an actual attack, not merely a feint.

At the next sortie, the warriors of Lean Bull recognized immediately the tactics now used and pressed closer. A shower of arrows flew from the attackers. Most fell short, but one lucky shot felled the horse of a lancer.

Quickly, the man stripped equipment from the dying animal, salvaging weapons, blankets, and water.

"Keep moving!" shouted Cabeza, reining back to help the fallen trooper.

A couple of warriors rode forward to intercept, but the lancer swung up behind Cabeza and he wheeled the black stallion back toward the main column. One warrior loosed an arrow in frustration, but it fell harmlessly short.

The lancer slid to the ground to join the party on foot. There were no extra horses.

"Sanchez!" called Garcia. "Give him your horse!"

Sanchez looked for a moment as if he were going to object, but then realized that the time was not appropriate to assert his claim to authority. He slid clumsily to the ground. The trooper vaulted to the saddle and swung the bay mare into position. The party continued to move without pause and the disgruntled Sanchez took his place among those on foot. He placed himself squarely between two of the crossbowmen. It should be safer there among professional soldiers than with the poorly armed servants. Self-consciously, Sanchez touched his sword. He had never used a sword. Mother of God, how had he ever allowed himself to become involved in this idiotic expedition?

The savages appeared to be preparing for another attack. Cabeza rode back down the column, shouting to close up the ranks. Then he pointed to a nearby creek bed, with a scattering of trees and broken rock which would offer some defensive possibilities.

"Over here! Keep moving! Close it up!"

The party swung in that direction and moved toward the stream. During this season, there was little water, except for deep holes and back eddies of the creek. The stream bed was half a man's height below the level of the plain and would offer good cover and partial concealment.

Cabeza swung the leading lancers aside as they reached their defensive position. They took up a protective stance to cover the retreat of the others. The people on foot reached the bank and started to jump and half stumble into its protective shelter. Sanchez and one of the crossbowmen clattered into a loose pile of white gravel and the soldier turned to place his weapon at the ready. The man dropped to his knees, methodically placed a heavy bolt in the channel of his already braced weapon, and assumed a firing position with elbows on the cutbank. Sanchez crowded as close to him as he could without attracting attention.

Now the last of the servants had tumbled into the protection of the creek bed. Half the crossbowmen turned and took up positions to protect the rear and the lancers reformed to present a solid line in front.

The savages were pushing forward now. Fascinated, Sanchez watched as the yipping, yelling warriors surged toward them.

At what seemed the last possible moment, Cabeza stood in his stirrups and waved his sword in the signal to attack. Side by side, he and Don Pedro Garcia led the platoon of lancers in a short charge to meet the yelling warriors.

Sanchez's heart rose in his throat. What if they rode too far out and the savages came around them? He gripped the hilt of his sword.

It was soon apparent that the lancers were not too far out in their defensive charge. The two groups met with a clash and the momentum of the savages carried the battle back toward the creek bed. Dust rose around the combatants. Sanchez saw Don Pedro expertly dodge the blow of a war club and thrust with his sword—and his adversary fell and lay still. An arrow whistled past and Sanchez ducked, long after it would have done any good.

He glanced at his companion and saw the crossbowman beside him, leaning over his weapon, sighting and seeking a target. No clear opportunity presented itself.

Then, out of the thickening dust of the melee, Sanchez saw Cabeza and a muscular warrior emerge. They were circling and sparring, coming closer to the cutbank. Still, the bowman had no clear shot.

The lieutenant was now crowding the other horseman, wielding his sword rapidly and pushing the warrior backward. Suddenly, the black stallion seemed to sag. His hindquarters sank and the knees buckled. With one last spasmodic lurch, the great horse fell and, for the first time, Sanchez could see a hand's span of feathered arrow shaft protruding from the animal's rib cage.

Cabeza attempted to kick free of the entangling stirrups, but one boot caught and he fell heavily, trying to free the encumbered leg. As he struggled, the other horseman circled and readied for the final blow. His heavy stone war club dangled, swinging, ready.

The scene seemed only an arm's length in front of him and Sanchez was frozen, immobilized by his inability to help. He kept expecting the bowman to loose his bolt. "Shoot, in Christ's name, shoot," he whispered. Still, nothing. He glanced at the other.

The soldier slumped over his crossbow in precisely the same position as before, the weapon aimed in the general direction of the battle. It took a long moment for Sanchez to notice that something was different. The man's posture was loose, his hands limp. Only then did Sanchez see the end of a feathered shaft jutting from the front of his tunic.

Panicky, he seized the weapon from lifeless hands and pointed it at the circling warrior. Cabeza still fought to free his left foot from beneath the dead animal.

Sanchez struggled with the unfamiliar weapon. He had never held one before. Now, how in Christ's name did they loose the bolt? Somewhere, there must be a lever or knob. Almost accidentally, the searching fingers of his right hand struck the release mechanism under the stock and there was a jarring twang. The crossbow bucked from the recoil and the deadly bolt leaped forward. Startled, Sanchez squealed in alarm and dropped the weapon, falling to his knees to cover his eyes with both hands.

A long moment later, he jerked his hands away. The warrior still sat on his horse, but his club now dangled loosely. He had turned and was now facing Sanchez, a confused, surprised look on his dark face. Slowly, he turned the horse and rode directly toward the stricken

Sanchez. Cabeza was free now and scrambling to his feet, shouting something.

Just as the warrior had almost reached the gully, where Sanchez stood frozen to the spot, he paused. The surprise in his eyes faded to incoherence and he tumbled limply to the ground. The horse bolted and ran back the way it had come.

Cabeza trotted over, weapon ready, but the man was quite dead. The lieutenant pointed with his sword to a small round hole in the right armpit, from which blood oozed slowly.

"Your bolt struck just as he raised his arm to use the club," he said wonderingly.

Cabeza was still visibly shaken by his close call, but not so badly as Sanchez. The little man could not speak, could hardly breathe in and out. He sank to a sitting position in the white gravel of the stream bed.

The sounds of combat were fading and Sergeant Perez trotted up to report that the savages were retreating. Cabeza nodded, still weak-kneed.

"They will be back, with more warriors."

23
>> >> >>

Night had fallen. The travelers had posted a heavy guard, though it was not thought that the savages would attack again. Small fires flickered. The hollow cry of an unfamiliar night bird was a sharp contrast to the moaning of the injured.

Cabeza threaded his way through the camp, pausing here and there to speak to a soldier or check on an animal. Casualties were heavy, though not so severe as he had feared at first. Two or three men down and bleeding look like half the platoon, he realized.

He passed the point where the body of his black stallion lay in the dim starlight a few steps away. A little further down the dry creek bed burned a tiny fire, where Don Pedro Garcia lounged. Cabeza clattered through the shifting white stones of the stream bed and sat beside the old man. Garcia looked up expectantly.

"Three horses dead, one missing. Three men, two more wounded."

"Badly?"

Cabeza nodded and sipped from the waterskin.

"One very bad. Won't live the night. The other has a lance wound—here."

He touched his left upper arm just below the shoulder.

"How many of them?"

"Who knows? They carry off their dead and wounded. It does not matter. They will bring more now."

Don Pedro acknowledged, seemingly unconcerned.

"Tell me, Ramon, is it true, what the men are saying? Did Sanchez really save your life?"

Cabeza nodded soberly. He had not fully recovered from the close encounter.

"It surely is! The other man was ready for the last blow and I was caught under my horse. It was close!"

Don Pedro chuckled and glanced up the creek to where Sanchez squatted with a couple of crossbowmen. He shook his head in disbelief.

"Remember that, Ramon. Men have strengths and weaknesses that do not show. You will see strong men whimper and weak men become heroes."

He shook his head and chuckled again.

"By Christ's blood! Sanchez!" he muttered, half to himself.

Don Pedro had emerged from the fight unscathed, but the story of his valor was unquestionably second to the story of Sanchez's remarkable feat. One of the bowmen had chanced to see the entire episode, as the frightened little man snatched the dead soldier's crossbow.

As the story was told and retold, it grew slightly in the telling. Sanchez became practically a hero. He was suddenly accepted without reservation by the bowmen, friends of the dead man. They took him as one of themselves and began to teach him the use of his newly acquired weapon. Sanchez was responding admirably, with restraint and some degree of awe.

"What about tomorrow?" Cabeza was greatly concerned.

Don Pedro shrugged. "Who knows? It may be the best fight of our lives!"

Yes, thought Cabeza. Or the last, more likely. It was virtually certain that the Head Splitters would have sent for reinforcements after the first abortive attack. He tried to estimate how long it might be until a messenger could go and return with other warriors. It would probably be noon tomorrow before they could arrive. Then the assault would begin. Then, or next morning. It would matter little.

Cabeza had racked his brain, but saw no clear solution. Theirs was a fairly defensible position. Water was accessible, but food was limited. The attacking force would be able to acquire both. He tried to guess how long they could hold out before they were picked off one at a time or succumbed to a final assault. Bad as their position had become, to attempt to improve it would make it worse. If they tried to move, they would be even more vulnerable.

The possibility that the warriors of Lean Bull would leave without a fight hardly seemed worth considering.

He was also concerned about the fighting strength of his party. They had lost three lancers, two dead and the one now moaning in the gully, mortally wounded. The other wounded man was a servant who had attempted to join the battle with a short sword. He had been simply outmanned. And, of course, the crossbowman, victim of a lucky shot, which was also nearly the death of Cabeza. He would have nightmares about that for a very long time.

Equally important to the living was the loss of the horses. With part of the party already on foot, the horses could become a critical element. They had now lost five animals. From a tactical standpoint, his force was now reduced by nearly one fourth already. Loss of another horse or two would cripple the lancer platoon. Cabeza wondered whether any of the packhorses could be ridden in an emergency. The present situation certainly represented such an emergency.

"*Señor* Garcia," the lieutenant tried once more, "you

are more experienced in such matters than I. What is to be done?"

The old don shrugged once more.

"Ramon," he began in a kindly and patient tone, "I have been in harder places."

Cabeza was afraid for a moment that the other was about to launch some of his endless and oft-repeated war stories. But it was not to be.

"We must take one day at a time. Something may happen to change things. Now I am going to sleep."

Now Cabeza was even more alarmed. It was apparent that Don Pedro did not intend to give him any help. He was irritated at this turn of events as he sought his blankets. He should be able to count on his superior officer to aid and support him. Don Pedro was acting as if there were not even a problem.

Suddenly, the whole truth sank home and the lieutenant sat bolt upright in shocked realization. The old warrior's mind must have slipped. What had appeared to be bravery during the day was more like a reflex action. Don Pedro, stressed constantly and concerned over the search for his son, had finally snapped. His tired brain had refused to accept the reality of failure for the mission. He had happily returned to relive the campaigns of his best years.

"Mother of God!" Cabeza whispered to himself. "*Señor* Garcia has gone mad!"

A chill gripped him as he rapidly recalled the events of the past day. He could not remember that Garcia had even mentioned the search since they had left the Head Splitters' village. True, there had been no occasion to, but Don Pedro was fond of talking about it anyway. Today, nothing. His entire approach to the current happenings had slipped in and out of reality with a detached military effectiveness. Complete professionalism as a soldier was the only emotion left. This was the reason, Cabeza now realized, that the old don had seemed relaxed, almost happy. He was doing the thing he loved and that which he had done best.

The realization did not help the troubled thoughts of Cabeza as he settled down for a sleepless night. The sudden sense of total responsibility for the doomed expedition was almost overwhelming.

It was some time later when he noticed that the moaning in the darkness upstream had ceased.

24
>> >> >>

Heads Off reined his gray mare toward the ridge. Perhaps from there he could see some sign. Sun Boy was overhead and they had found no sign of the travelers or of the Head Splitters.

This was a matter of some concern. If the information brought by the girl, South Wind, were correct, the travelers would have been attacked last night. Even though they had been warned, they might have been killed.

The plan of the war party of the People was simple. They knew approximately where the first night camp of the travelers was to have been. The direction of travel was north and it was decided to move so as to cut the trail of the travelers to the north of the night camp. Then, with the plain track of the moving party before them, they could follow rapidly and assist in whatever way they could.

It had seemed a logical plan, but something had gone wrong. In some way, they had missed the trail of the moving strangers. Heads Off was certain they had not crossed it. Both Long Elk and Standing Bird were excellent trackers and both had seen nothing. Either the travelers had taken another direction for the day's travel or they had been killed in the sneak attack in the night.

Overlooked was the fact that they might be alive but pinned down, unable to move. Thus, the People had passed to the north of the beleaguered party.

Scouts could be sent out, but it was known that Head Splitters were in the area in strength. The scouts would be at great risk, alone and badly outnumbered. They should probably be no further out than to act as outriders to the main force.

Heads Off fretted and chafed under the frustration involved. Time was an important factor. Already, they were a day later in starting than he wished. The party of strangers had been forced to make their initial defense alone.

He turned in the saddle and beckoned to Long Elk, who cantered forward.

"What now, my brother? You have been this way. Where do you think they are?"

Long Elk shrugged.

"We should have crossed their back trail by now. Maybe they turned west."

"Then we should move south to find them?"

"I think so. Maybe we will find their back trail there."

South Wind came loping up to the two men. She had insisted on accompanying the war party.

"My chief!" she sounded urgent. "We have missed them somewhere!"

The men nodded and Long Elk spoke.

"Yes, little one. We turn south to try to find their trail. They may have turned west from the night camp."

"But they may not have!"

She turned to Heads Off.

"My chief, we should go to their last camp! We can read the sign and follow their trail!"

It was so obvious a solution that it had been overlooked. Return to the last location of the missing party.

"South Wind, do you know where they planned to camp?"

"Of course. It is the only good camp within a sleep of here."

"Lead the way, then."

He raised an arm and signaled the change in direction. The girl set out at a good stiff lope until finally Long Elk cautioned her.

"*Aiee*, little sister! If we kill our elk-dogs with speed, we are on foot again!"

Heads Off had begun to sense urgency in the attitude of the girl. There must be something not apparent, that she was so concerned over a group of strangers. He rode up beside her, as they walked the horses to rest them.

"South Wind, tell me more of these Hairfaces."

"There is little to tell, my chief. What did you wish?"

"Why should you care about these strangers? They are of no good to you."

The girl's eyes filled with tears. She had endured much and had slept little for the past two days. She blurted her story.

"My chief, there is one of the Hairfaces called Rahmone. He is their war chief and he is special to me. We have good medicine together. I am afraid for his life."

She paused, embarrassed.

"There is the old man, too," she continued. "He may be your father!"

He wished to hear more. His mind had reeled in confusion ever since he had heard of the Hairfaces' party. Heads Off had become so thoroughly one of the People that he felt detached. Still, when he heard of people from his previous life, there was a tug of sentimental memory. Sometimes, he felt as if he were two different people. He must know more of these strangers.

"Tell me, South Wind. Do you think this man is my father? What does he look like?"

"I do not know, my chief. He is tall and old. His hair is as white as that of White Buffalo, the medicine man. The fur on his face is white, also."

She gave a quick side glance and a self-conscious little smile.

"I did not know that would be so. He carries a very big knife that shines in the sunlight."

Her spread hands indicated what must be a sword.

So far, the physical description could be Don Pedro Garcia. It could also fit a thousand other men.

"Do they ride elk-dogs?"

"Of course. The white-fur rides a gray mare, like yours."

Correct again, he thought, but still, there are many gray horses.

"How is he called?"

She shook her head.

"I do not know. Their words are strange to my ears. I cannot remember the sounds."

"Except for Rah-mone," observed Long Elk, who was listening.

The girl blushed and smiled.

"Yes, tell us more of this Rah-mone."

"He is tall, nearly as tall as you, my chief. His fur is like yours. He rides a big black elk-dog and carries the big knife instead of a spear."

Ah, thought Heads Off. An officer.

"What do his warriors carry?"

"Spears, mostly. The ones with spears ride elk-dogs. About this many."

She held up fingers, first both hands, then one.

"Some walk and carry a strange weapon. It is a short bow, tied to a big stick. It throws a little arrow, very hard."

Heads Off nodded.

"Any others?"

"Only those who carry supplies. One or two others."

So, he concluded, a platoon of lancers, a short squad of crossbowmen, and a contingent of servants. From the description, a well-equipped expedition. The name Rah-mone meant nothing to him.

Their mounts were now rested somewhat and they resumed a ground-eating steady canter. It was nearly time to slow to a walk again, when Red Dog, scouting ahead, suddenly turned at the top of a hill and signaled the party forward.

The main group held back to allow the trackers to examine the abandoned campsite. Piles of fluffy white ashes marked the campfires, abandoned only since daylight.

Had there been a fight? Yes, Standing Bird reported. Probably before dawn. Several had been killed or wounded, judging from bloodstains on the grass in several places.

"Mostly Head Splitters," observed Long Elk.

Heads Off was astounded.

"How do you know that?"

"There are no bodies. The Head Splitters took them away."

He pointed south, then turned to indicate a plain trail headed north.

"Hairfaces went that way."

Long Elk shrugged as if any child could read such sign and pointed to the horse tracks crossing a soft area. All were of uniform depth, none markedly different from the others.

"No elk-dogs with double loads. No bodies."

Heads Off had not realized the relief such a find would bring. At least, the party had been alive and traveling this morning.

The girl, too, appeared much more optimistic as they turned north again on the trail.

The trackers were in the lead and soon Standing Bird returned to report that the travelers were being harassed by a small war party of Head Splitters. Trampled places in the tall grass were seen, where a defensive circle had been formed. There were a few stray arrows near three places, but no blood or evidence of a fight.

Late in the afternoon, Long Elk signaled. He had found a dead horse, a well-built gray, with an arrow jutting from the upper neck. It had been killed only today.

"Hair-face's horse," observed Standing Bird, pointing to the shiny military saddle.

Heads Off was more interested in the dead animal. He examined it for some time, then suggested that someone salvage the saddle, and the group moved on. Long Elk, who had discovered the horse, was given the honor of removing the saddle. He immediately gave away his old saddle pad to one of the younger Elk-dog men and the group moved on.

Sun Boy's torch was sinking when Standing Bird again came back to advise caution. They had discovered that the track ahead was all but obliterated by the tracks of a large number of horsemen. The pursuers of the fleeing party had been joined by more warriors than two men have fingers and toes.

It was decided to camp for the night. It would be madness to pursue a large force of the enemy in darkness in his own country.

There was much frustration, but none quite so severe as that experienced by Heads Off. He was the only one present whose knowledge enabled him to read the entire story of the dead horse. He was the only one of the People who understood the importance of the scar on the animal's shoulder. It was a brand, the gracefully shaped identifying mark placed with a hot iron on the left shoulder of every Andalusian stallion in the stables of Don Pedro Garcia.

25

» » »

Lean Bull lay stretched on his robe, propped on an elbow so that he could observe the twinkling of the distant fires. He had no desire to sleep. It had been a day of frustration.

Once more he had been thwarted in his effort to crush the young war chief of the Hairfaces. It should have been possible, even easy, to attack the column successfully. Instead, he had lost more warriors.

He felt the slipping of prestige among his followers. It would be necessary to accomplish an overwhelming victory, with many honors counted and many horses captured, to restore his respect.

Lean Bull felt that it had been no more than luck which had enabled the strangers to retreat into the stream bed and make their defense. His mind refused to accept that it could have been good strategy and planning on the part of the young chief.

He did have to admit to the bravery of the Hairfaces. He had been amazed at the charge of the old white-hair, shouting and swinging the long knife. The white-haired chief, it seemed, was experienced in battle.

Lean Bull regretted deeply the loss of the black stallion. He had seen, from a distance, the animal go down and its rider pinned beneath. He was furious, as he had plainly told the entire party that the young chief, as well as the black horse, belonged to Lean Bull. The young warrior with ideas of his own had paid dearly for his initiative. The Head Splitters were still amazed at the efficiency of the strange short weapon used by the crossbowmen.

Lean Bull had tried to reach the place where the young hair-face was unhorsed, but was unable to do so. Then the fight had swept away from the gully and it seemed impractical to make another attack.

No matter. The strangers had lost men, too. At least three, he thought. The spearmen had been struck the hardest, because they had been in the thick of the defense while the others had scrambled for cover.

Lean Bull glanced at the stars and estimated the time until Sun Boy's awakening. The coming sun would see the end of the Hairfaces.

He had carefully studied the terrain before darkness fell. The strangers' position was secure against a small force. They could turn back attacks by Lean Bull's war party. They could find cover behind the cutbank and water in the deeper holes of the creek bed. They had food and, if necessary, could eat their own horses. Such a group might hold out for many sleeps.

But against a larger war party, they could not survive. The defenders could not meet an attack from both sides. There were simply not enough men.

Lean Bull was tempted to divide his party and attack at dawn. Surely, he could overrun the position of the Hairfaces. Prudence held him back, however. He must make certain that the first attack was a success. He questioned whether his warriors would follow him in a second try.

So, they must wait for reinforcements. He had sent word back to the tribe after the failure of surprise in the night camp. There were many aspiring young warriors who would be eager to follow the great Lean Bull into battle.

He estimated that by noon, with Sun Boy's torch overhead, he would have four times as many warriors as the little group in the gully. Then they would attack from both sides at once. It would soon be over.

He rather hated to share the honors. Much better, had he been able to lead his party to victory without help. If there were only some way to force the defenders out into the open. There, Lean Bull and his horsemen could cut them to pieces almost at leisure. He had racked his brain, but could think of no possible means to accomplish this. The Hairfaces were firmly rooted in the confines of the stream bed.

For a brief time, Lean Bull considered setting fire to the tall grass along the gully. A quick look, however, assured him that the growth was too green to burn. He would be forced to wait.

So, Lean Bull reclined on his robe and fretted, waiting for two things to occur. The first would be the coming of the sun. This would enable him to scout more precisely the condition of the defenders and to determine how best to make the attack.

Second, he must wait for the other warriors from the village. They would be already on the way, he realized. Some might travel through the night. So, the first of the reinforcements might arrive by midmorning. The main body would be present by noon and Lean Bull had already, in his mind, set this as the time for the final attack.

He glanced again at the stars, watching the Seven Hunters swing around their lodge at the Real-star. Time was passing so slowly. Lean Bull was anxious to meet, in individual hand-to-hand combat, the young war chief who had embarrassed him. He was still smarting over the matter of the girl. She was not now available as the object of his vengeance. He would have to be content to vent his wrath on the other half of the pair who had shamed him. Lean Bull's grasp tightened on the handle of his war club and his teeth clenched in rage. He must make certain that no one else reached the young hair-face first. Lean Bull alone must be the one to count honors in the defeat of the hair-faced young chief.

He sighed deeply and rolled over. Suddenly he sat bolt upright, staring to the west.

There, in the far distance, something was blotting out the starry sky. For some distance above the earth's rim, a dense and growing blackness, deeper than the night's dome, came mushrooming up, obscuring the twinkling lights of the stars.

Even as Lean Bull watched, there was a flicker of orange heat lightning across the face of the cloud bank, next to the horizon. He almost laughed aloud. Again the orange shadow flitted across the blue-blackness of the storm front. This time he noted a tiny streak of real-fire, darting down and stabbing at the earth's surface. Long moments later came the muted rumble of distant thunder, so soft that he would not even have been aware of it if he had not been watching the play of the lightning.

Now he chuckled openly. He could not have planned it better. He had wished for a means to force the defenders up and out of the stream bed. Now, as if in answer to his wish, came one of the summer storms common to the prairie.

Relaxed now, almost happy with anticipation, Lean Bull watched the storm sweep toward them. It might be his best ally now in the fulfilling of his revenge.

26

>> >> >>

In the uncomfortable camp in the dry stream bed, Sanchez tossed miserably in his blankets. He was frightened. Things had become worse and worse, the further the expedition had gone. For the thousandth time, he cursed himself for his greed. How, by all that was holy, could he possibly have fabricated a tale that had brought this entire party to perish on the plains of this godforsaken continent?

For, as nearly as he could see, perish they must. The lieutenant had already told them that the savages were only waiting for reinforcements. Then, sometime after dawn tomorrow, would come the assault. Probably from all sides, Cabeza had said.

Sanchez was terrified at the thought that this would probably be the last sunrise of his miserable life. It made things no better that he was considered a hero since the fight. Try as he would to maintain his composure, he was certain that his terror would be apparent to all.

He was a hero only by virtue of a freak accident. He could still not believe that he had actually picked up the weapon of the dead soldier, discharged it, and killed the attacking warrior. To the others, none of his protests seemed to make any difference. They could not realize his ineptness, his unreasoning, irrational behavior. They saw only the man who had, in an emergency, acted to save the life of their lieutenant.

To be sure, Sanchez was enjoying their newfound friendship. He was being treated almost as an equal by the crossbowmen. He was basking in this new respect, but it, too, could become a problem. He would now be expected to perform in combat with a skill equal to his accidental achievement of the previous battle. This, Sanchez was certain, was an impossibility. He doubted that his two legs would even hold him up when the attack came.

In the midst of all this troubled thought, Sanchez heard a far-off mutter of thunder. It was the darkest hour before the dawn, his mind was exhausted, and for some time the significance did not filter into his consciousness. Thunder rumbled again in the distance.

Within minutes, the sound was closer—and each flash of lightning brighter and closer. Puffs of wind stirred the trees along the creek and a light rain began to fall.

Up and down the creek bed, men scrambled for blankets and scraps of canvas to shelter their heads from the increasing downpour. Sanchez felt soaked to the skin. Water squished in his boots as he shifted uncomfortably in the dark.

Perhaps because he was already so wet, he did not at first realize that the water was rising. There was a slight tug of current at his ankles, a subtle shifting of the sand and gravel beneath his boot soles.

Almost at the same instant, Sanchez heard a distant rushing and roaring sound. A man upstream shouted a warning, but the rush of water was upon them. Sanchez was nearly knocked from his feet. A horse splashed past him, lunging toward the higher ground. Frantically, he clutched what equipment fell to his hands and scrambled over the low bank.

"Over here! Over here!" Cabeza was shouting.

A flickering flash of lightning showed for an instant a cluster of men and horses, stumbling to join together for mutual defense. The next instant, all was darkness again. Sanchez started to run in that direction and collided with a frightened horse. Almost by reflex alone he grabbed at the animal's dangling rope. The horse followed along with him.

Another flashing lightning bolt showed him slightly off course. He had nearly stepped into the swollen creek. Ahead, Sanchez could hear the confusion of the main group, as sodden survivors clustered and clung together.

It seemed an eternity before the dull gray daylight began to lighten the leaden overcast. The storm slowly moved on to the east, rumbling and flashing in the distance. The rain had stopped, except for a fine mist that seemed to hang in the air. Sanchez thought he had never been so thoroughly soaked. Somehow even the light drizzle now falling seemed wetter than the deluge that had produced the flash flood.

The sodden little group of survivors huddled together on the stream bank. Any semblance of cover or concealment had now vanished under the rushing torrent behind them. Cabeza moved among the men, trying to take stock of the situation.

Two men were missing, presumably drowned. Most of their equipment and part of their weapons had been swept away. Of the horses, only a scant half dozen remained.

The most terrifying aspect, however, as the gray dawn slowly increased visibility, was their exposed position. The little group huddled on the higher of the stream banks. Water spread across the meadow on the opposite shore, rushing among the trees and rocks where they had found shelter. Here, in the open, was nothing. They could retreat only a few steps and their movement was blocked by the bank-high torrent.

Cabeza pointed upstream. A few hundred paces away was a cluster of a half dozen scrubby trees. They were poorly seen in the dim light, but they offered the only possibility of cover of any sort on this side of the stream. The dripping survivors, like so many half-drowned rats, straggled in that direction.

Before they had reached the trees, a trio of warriors made a mock rush at them. They stayed well out of weapon range. It seemed likely that they were merely scouts, probing to discover the extent of the storm's damage to their intended quarry. Apparently satisfied, they withdrew.

Sanchez glanced at the lieutenant, wondering if he had noticed the same thing that he, Sanchez, had. In his terror of the attacking force, he had realized that now the warriors could attack from only one direction. The flooded creek, while placing them in an exposed position, had also eliminated the possibility of a flanking attack from the other shore. A moment later, Sanchez assured himself that of course Cabeza knew this. It was his job to know. Furthermore, he saw, as they straggled into the tiny cluster of trees, that it was a natural site for a last-ditch defense.

The little grove—some type of oaks, it seemed—was located on a point of land which jutted out into the creek bed. Undoubtedly, this very patch of tough, gnarled growth had helped to divert the course of the stream over the years. Soil held by a tangle of roots is more resistant to the erosive action of water. The result was this higher tongue of land, with the stream circling around it. By sheer good fortune, the flooded creek now gave protection in an arc that covered nearly two thirds of their perimeter. The point was far more defensible than it had originally seemed.

Sanchez slumped in among the trees and dropped the oddly assorted equipment he carried to tie the horse to a tree. He was glad for respite from the threat of immediate death from the arrows or clubs of the Head Splitters. He felt almost secure for a moment as he sank down to rest, as near the protection of the creek's rushing current as he could get. Let the others take positions near the attack point!

He glanced behind him and wondered how long the water would run high. When the flood began to recede, they would again be vulnerable to attack from all sides.

27
» » »

Ramon Cabeza watched the sun struggle to break through the thinning cloud cover. Scraps of blue sky appeared for a short time, only to be overrun again by the shifting and overlapping patches of gray. The atmosphere was hot, steamy, and uncomfortable.

In the heavy grass in front of their position, droplets of water sparkled like jewels in the occasional ray of sunlight which broke through. A misty haze of steam rose and hung over the little valley, unmoving in the still morning air. It lent an unreality to the distant figures of Lean Bull and his warriors. They moved about, squatted, or mounted to ride up and down the hill with arrogant pride. It was apparent that their purpose was to impress the defenders in the little cluster of trees.

Cabeza was impressed. The situation had deteriorated so rapidly in the past two days that he could hardly believe it. The expedition had left the Head Splitters' village in strength and confidence only two mornings ago. Now they were reduced to barely more than half strength, had lost all their supplies and most of their horses. They had hardly enough weapons to mount a defense of any sort when the final rush came. Cabeza hoped that the warriors of Lean Bull did not realize the helplessness of their victims' plight.

Not that it would make much difference. The Head Splitters could probably overrun the little party of travelers at any time, with no more men than they already had. But he was certain they were waiting for more warriors from the main camp. Then the assault would come. His main hope now was that his party would be able to show respectable strength in their own final defense.

What was it his instructor at the Academy had once said?

"When the situation becomes hopeless, to die well is the final insult to one's enemy."

Something like that. Cadet Ramon Cabeza had not listened well. In his youthful exuberance, he had not for an instant believed that he would ever find himself in a situation that had become hopeless. That sort of thing was for others.

Now he sat in the mud of the prairie near the center of the vast new continent, about to be overrun by savages. Poorly armed savages, at that, by modern standards. Their weapons were chipped from the stone of their hillsides, but he had been forced to respect their expertise. The warriors of Lean Bull had systematically whittled away at the strength of the expedition, until now they were reduced to a pitiful handful, poorly armed, with little leadership except for his own.

Cabeza glanced over at Don Pedro Garcia. The old man was sleeping peacefully. In a brief conversation earlier, it had become more apparent that his mind had slipped yet further. With bright, burning enthusiasm, the old don had outlined strategy for the coming battle.

"We must deploy a squadron of lancers," he pointed at the distant ridge, "and then bring the artillery up behind. The dragoons can sweep up from the south, with the foot troops following!"

Sound strategy, Cabeza had to admit. It fit the terrain perfectly and would put the enemy at a decided disadvantage. There was only one simple flaw in the plan. Merely that there was no squadron of lancers, no artillery or dragoons, and no foot troops. Merely the bedraggled handful of survivors on the muddy point of land in the bend of the flooded creek.

He looked at Sanchez, who waved and smiled. Ah, Sanchez. The man had never openly admitted it, but Cabeza had long assumed that the other had no real knowledge of the prairie. He must have conceived this entire expedition for personal glorification and enrichment. How unfortunate that his folly had carried so many others along with him.

Yet this same unlikely little man had shown unexpected strength. He had actually saved Cabeza's life. His life had been saved twice in as many days, the lieutenant reflected moodily. The other time, it was the slim girl who had become such a part of his thoughts. He wondered where she might be and if she had managed to return to her people. She would undoubtedly marry one of her own and raise children. They would be strong warriors, he had no doubt.

Gloomily, he wondered if she would remember him. Would she ever tell her children of the hair-faced stranger who had entered her life for a short while?

The girl, he had decided, was the key to Lean Bull's determination. Originally, the Head Splitter may have been seeking to steal the goods and supplies of the travelers. Now it was more than that. It had become a personal thing, a vendetta to avenge what Lean Bull considered an affront to his dignity.

Slowly, an idea began to dawn. Could it be that Lean Bull considered this a private matter, to the extent that he would accept a personal challenge? There was nothing to lose, Cabeza reflected. The little group was doomed anyway. Perhaps he could bargain for their lives. He was unfamiliar with native custom, but it might be worth a try. He turned to consult with Lizard.

The interpreter was squatting near Sanchez, trying in vain to kindle a fire. It was hopeless, with all combustible material soaking wet, and the young native cast aside the sodden mess just as Cabeza approached.

"Lizard," he began, with signs and a mixtnre of Spanish and native words, "would the Head Splitter chief fight me instead of killing the whole group?"

The interpreter shrugged.

"Who knows? My people would. Of them, I do not know. You could ask them."

The parlay must be immediate, Cabeza thought. If the main party of warriors arrived, it would be much more difficult to negotiate. The sun had just succeeded in displacing the mist and cloud cover. There was now a light breeze beginning to stir the drying grasses when the young lieutenant of lancers rode out into the meadow. Lizard trotted at his side.

There was a flurry of activity among the Head Splitters on the hill and Lean Bull swung up to his horse's back, to walk slowly forward. Other warriors joined him, but the chief motioned them back. He pointed to one man and they advanced, side by side.

Cabeza had stopped, at Lizard's suggestion, in the center of the meadow. He sat still on the horse, right hand raised in salute. The others approached and stopped.

Cabeza nodded a greeting.

"We meet again," he gestured.

"One last time."

"My chief," Cabeza came directly to the point, "will you fight me and let the others go?"

To his surprise, Lean Bull laughed aloud.

"I will kill you and then kill the others!"

"But if I win," Cabeza persisted, "they go free?"

Lean Bull chuckled.

"That will not be."

"But if it is, if I kill you, then your warriors will let them go?"

Lean Bull nodded impatiently.

"Tell him, then."

Cabeza motioned to the other warrior. Lean Bull turned and spoke rapidly. It was impossible to know whether he was giving honest instructions.

"When will this fight be?"

Lean Bull shrugged, then pointed overhead.

"When the sun is straight up."

Cabeza nodded and turned his horse, deliberately exposing his back to the other, and rode calmly back toward the little clump of trees.

28
>> >> >>

All morning, warriors of Lean Bull's tribe had been trickling into the area, by twos and threes and handfuls. Only a short while ago, the largest party yet had arrived, swelling the mass of milling warriors by dozens.

Now the sun was almost directly overhead and Cabeza tightened his girth and prepared to mount. He had chosen one of the gray Garcia stallions, the one that appeared the best and most maneuverable. He handed the reins to one of the lancers and stepped over to speak to Don Pedro for a moment.

The old man was seated, facing the meadow, talking intensely to himself. His eyes glittered with excitement and his hands fluttered nervously in his lap.

"I go now, *Señor* Garcia."

Don Pedro barely glanced up and there was not the slightest hint of recognition in the nervously shifting old eyes. He continued to mutter and babble incoherently. Cabeza sighed deeply and clasped a hand on the old warrior's shoulder.

"God be with you, *señor*."

With a frustrated sigh, he rose to return to his horse. He swung to the saddle and turned to speak to the lancers.

The bearded sergeant had brought the platoon forward as if for inspection. Their once splendid blue and white uniforms, now disheveled and dirty, had been made as presentable as possible. Only the sergeant and four others still possessed a horse, but these were drawn up with military precision. Behind them, the other lancers stood at attention on foot, with weapons at ready.

The sergeant saluted smartly and Cabeza returned the gesture. Pride in his platoon brought a lump to his throat. It was just as well, he reflected, that he would not be required to speak. It was better to cover the emotion of the moment with the formality of a military salute.

Cabeza turned the stallion and kneed the animal briskly forward into the meadow. Mounted warriors surged down from the hill and arranged themselves in a half circle around the level area.

Lean Bull strutted forward, face painted for battle. His horse, too, was decorated with geometric designs and crimson handprints on the chest and flanks. He carried a circular shield of rawhide and his heavy stone war club dangled ready in his right hand.

Cabeza had chosen the saber as his weapon. There had been no rules established. None were necessary. It would be a fight to the death. Then it would remain to be seen whether the followers of Lean Bull would honor the terms of the challenge.

The two warriors circled and Cabeza drew his sword and prepared for a run at the other. With military precision, he aligned the blade with his forearm and braced his right elbow. The stallion leaped forward at a touch of the spur. Lean Bull gave a yipping war cry and kicked his horse into a canter, swinging his great club in an arc around his head.

Cabeza directed the point of his blade at the bare midriff of the other and braced for the shock along his arm. At the same time, he ducked low under the whirling arc of the club. It was with some surprise that he felt the shock of contact diverted. Lean Bull had swung the iron-hard rawhide shield into position and the point of the sword slid harmlessly aside.

Now off-balance, Cabeza whirled his horse and prepared for the rush of the other. He managed to avoid the swing of the club again, but his slash with the blade once more clanged off the shield. Cabeza was becoming alarmed. It was all he could do to avoid the swing of the other's weapon. To do so placed him at a disadvantage in each encounter. He could not bring his sword into play while ducking, dodging, and bending, off-balance in the saddle. When he did manage to offer a return blow, the blade merely clanged against the shield of Lean Bull.

Cabeza was tiring rapidly. His predicament was brought sharply to his attention when a narrow miss by the stone club actually brushed the hair above his left ear. He must do something quickly.

He must attack Lean Bull's horse. Much as he disliked such tactics, Cabeza was fighting for his life and those of his companions. He had been completely unable to reach his opponent with any sort of effectiveness. But if he could put the horse down, there might be a chance that he could gain an advantage.

The opponents wheeled after another clash and the lieutenant heard a sudden shout behind him. He was looking directly at Lean Bull's face at that moment and saw blank astonishment appear as the warrior looked past him toward the creek. Cabeza spurred quickly aside and turned to look.

From the makeshift campsite at the little grove, a wild-eyed figure staggered, roaring his challenge. Don Pedro Garcia, hatless, disheveled white hair blowing in the wind, charged across the meadow on foot, bellowing and swinging his heavy sword.

Sergeant Perez spurred forward to intercept the deranged old man, but dared not come too close to the whirling blade. Two more lancers rode forward to assist and a scattering of foot soldiers and Garcia retainers straggled after.

To the Head Splitters on the slope, it must have appeared that the ragtag platoon at the creek was trying to mount an attack. Suddenly, the entire situation deteriorated into deadly confusion.

Cabeza attempted to yell that it was a mistake, but his shout was drowned in a chorus of yipping war cries. The line of mounted warriors broke and poured forward, lances and war clubs waving overhead. He wheeled the horse and ran, hearing the thunder behind him, watching his pitiful platoon attempt to form a defensive front as he approached.

He yanked the gray stallion to a sliding stop and pivoted to face the oncoming rush. With the precision of trained professionals, the handful of lancers swung into their short defensive charge. The two forces clashed, horses and men went down in a melee of confusion. The tangle swept toward the creek and the crossbowmen began to make themselves felt. Short, heavy crossbow bolts twanged, taking deadly toll.

Cabeza slashed, parried, thrust, and circled, trying to catch sight of Don Pedro. From the corner of his vision, he saw a lancer struck down, to fall heavily from his horse. One of the others vaulted to the saddle to bring his lance into play. A young warrior loomed before him, swinging his stone club. Cabeza readied his sword, but the other man's horse suddenly screamed and bucked away, unseating the rider. There was the brief glimpse of a crossbow bolt, projecting from the flank of the frantic animal, before it floundered away in the confusion.

Another lancer went down, trampled under the hooves of a painted warrior's horse. It could not last much longer. More warriors were pounding across the meadow, anxious to count honors before the last Hairfaces fell. The yipping falsetto war cry blended into a continuous high-pitched roar.

29
» » »

Heads Off, frustrated and tired, suddenly stopped his horse and held up a hand for silence. The straggling war party came to a halt, as everyone strained to listen.

Since dawn, when the sudden brief rain had blotted out all traces of the trail they were following, they had floundered. The general direction of travel had been north, so they maintained that course, but the scouts had seen nothing, beyond the occasional broken twig or trampled tuft of grass that indicated that someone or something had passed.

Now, in the silence of the halt, free from the shuffling and clopping noises of travel, others began to hear the sound. In the far distance, somewhere to their left, came the distinct sounds of battle. There were shouts, cries, a scream, and, swelling over all, the high falsetto *yip-yip-yip* of the Head Splitters' war cry.

The young chief reined his gray mare around and

started up the slope. Just at that moment, Standing Bird, who had been scouting in that direction, came charging down the ridge at a fast lope, waving excitedly. They hurried to meet the excited scout.

"They are attacking the Hairfaces by the creek! It is almost over!"

Quickly, Heads Off rode to the summit of the ridge. Before him, like a panorama in miniature, lay the scene of battle. Yipping, painted warriors pressed forward from all directions toward a tiny band of defenders backed against the bend of the flooded creek.

The remnants of a platoon in blue and white uniforms retreated with disciplined precision. Only three of the lancers were still mounted, he saw. It must have been deadly fighting. The other soldiers were fighting on foot, retreating step by step, attempting to defend the assortment of people on foot. The uninjured assisted the wounded toward the doubtful shelter of a few scrubby trees at the creek's edge.

One of the soldiers still on his horse was a tall young officer, who seemed to be everywhere at once. He reined up and down the hottest part of the line of battle, wielding his sword with great skill. Naturally, he was becoming the target of every aspiring young warrior. Heads Off marveled that the man was still in the saddle.

Quickly, Heads Off made tactical decisions, turning to the waiting warriors.

"Red Dog! Take your Bloods to the south end of the ridge! The rest spread out and follow me!"

In the meadow below, the jubilant Head Splitters, the scent of victory in their nostrils, were suddenly astonished by a new development. Above the din of battle came the deep full-throated rumble of the war cry of the People.

The followers of Lean Bull turned in surprise, to see the skyline of the ridge alive with motion. Painted horsemen, lances braced, poured over the hill to join in the battle. It was a sight to chill the blood of the most experienced warrior. For many of these, it was their first war party.

A youngster near the outside of the crowd turned and fled in panic, soon followed by another. The older warriors shouted in vain to stand fast. In the space of a few heartbeats, pandemonium reigned; the majority of Lean Bull's force was in full flight, followed by their frustrated leaders. Straight down the level strip of prairie along the creek they streamed, fearfully glancing back at the attacking force. Many were still looking over their shoulders when they reached the south end of the ridge and the waiting Blood Society under Red Dog's command.

The Bloods were aware that theirs was an important task. Their position placed them squarely in the escape route of the Head Splitter war party. They might be sorely tested, yet they were proud that their chief showed confidence in them.

For many years, it would be told in song and story around the council fires of the People. This was the event which for all time vindicated the Bloods and welcomed them back to full status in the tribe. Many honors would be counted this day.

Back at the meadow, the astounded defenders in the creek bend watched the wave of warriors come to their assistance. The former attackers were now fleeing in disorder.

Then, out of the thinning dust and confusion of battle, straight toward the spot where Cabeza sat on his sweating stallion, came Lean Bull. It was apparent that for him the battle was not over. The cause was lost and the only way to save face was to die bravely and try to take his enemy with him.

Cabeza ducked under the first rush and countered with the sword. Lean Bull swung the club with a vicious backhand sweep and struck the lieutenant's weapon near the hilt. The shock traveled up his arm to the shoulder and the sword went flying to the ground.

The Head Splitter turned triumphantly and readied the great club for another blow.

Cabeza threw himself from his horse and rolled, scrambling to regain his weapon.

"Here!"

A shout came from the sergeant, who tossed his lance to the man on foot. Cabeza whirled to face the coming charge. The pounding hooves of the warriors from the ridge were drawing nearer, but the two locked in personal combat could not turn to look.

"Rah-mone!"

Not until he heard South Wind's cry did Lean Bull turn. For the first time, he now seemed to notice the approaching horde.

"I will kill you later, hair-face," he signed.

Deliberately, he turned his horse away and sent the animal into the flooded stream, lunging toward higher ground on the opposite shore.

The girl had already vaulted from her horse and was running to Cabeza's arms.

Heads Off pulled his gray mare to a stop and slid down to approach the lieutenant. There was something familiar about the young officer, recalled from a distant place and time. His head whirled, as he tried to recall.

"Cabeza?" he asked hesitantly.

The other stood numbly, an arm around the girl. He stared at the tall, bronzed savage, smeared with war paint and carrying a stone-tipped lance. Only one thing seemed ludicrously out of place. The young chief who had led the charge down the ridge wore a full black beard.

"Mother of God," breathed the lieutenant. "Juan Garcia!"

30

» » »

Heads Off sat on the ground, partially supporting the head and shoulders of his father, Don Pedro Garcia. In the first rush of the Head Splitters, a warrior's weapon had found its mark. The old veteran had received a wound through the right upper chest from a buffalo lance.

His party had managed to carry and drag the wounded Don Pedro to the scant shelter of the trees. There he had remained for the rest of the fight, at times gasping for breath, at times only partly conscious. Still, it had been necessary to restrain him to prevent his trying to join the battle.

To the amazement of the two servants trying to administer to him, the old man awoke from one episode of semiconsciousness perfectly lucid and rational. Apparently, the shock of his wound had restored his mind to reason.

Now, although he was very weak, he appeared to understand the entire sequence of events. He had immediately recognized Juan, now Heads Off of the People. Like any other father, he was ready to glow with pride at the accomplishments of his son. He tried to shrug off the seriousness of his wound.

"Only a scratch! I have had much worse!"

Cabeza amd Heads Off exchanged sober glances. Both had seen the bloody sputum when the old warrior had coughed. There was also no denying the appearance of the chest wound. Whenever the clumsy bandage was removed, pink-tinged froth bubbled from the ragged gash. It was a severe injury to the lung and it appeared that there continued to be internal bleeding. The outlook was not good.

Heads Off had been almost constantly at his side. The two talked intermittently, Don Pedro relating news of home and of *Doña* Isabel. Heads Off responded with news of his own activities. He related how he had been lost and injured, how his departure had been repeatedly delayed, and how he had eventually married.

"You have two grandsons, father! They are fine boys."

He stumbled a little over the names of the youngsters. He was having a bit of difficulty thinking in Spanish after so long a time. And, oddly, he had never heard or spoken the names of his sons, Eagle and Little Owl, in any but the language of the People.

Heads Off related how he had received his own name, while still under observation by scouts of the People. The observers had never seen a helmet and the stranger had appeared to remove his head. Both men chuckled, but this set off a paroxysm of coughing for Don Pedro which was a matter of great concern for a few moments.

When he had quieted somewhat, the conversation resumed. Heads Off related the circumstances of the People's acquisition of horses, how the "elk-dogs" had changed their way of living. He, Juan, had had a part in the establishment of elk-dog medicine, the means

by which the animals were trained and controlled
The iron bit worn in the mouth of the gray mare
had assumed an almost religious significance in the
tribe.

Then there had come the time when the Southern
band of the People were leaderless. Their chief had
been killed in the Great Battle, and none of the young
chiefs of the band had the leadership experience to
assume the office. With many misgivings, Heads Off
had consented to lead the young men, who were now
becoming expert horsemen.

"Yes," nodded the older man, "that is true, my son
Your charge from the ridge was magnificent!"

Don Pedro was becoming very tired and Heads Off
urged him to rest. He did his best to make the old
man comfortable and then went to search for Cabeza

The lieutenant had finished an assessment of the
party's condition. Of the thirty-two who had stepped
off the *Paloma* weeks before, only sixteen remained
alive. Several of the survivors were badly wounded
The lancers had taken the brunt of the attack, but the
bowmen had lost two more men and the Garcia ser
vants had likewise been reduced in number. Lizard
was unscathed, though for a time it had appeared that
he might be in danger from both groups of warriors
Since he was unknown to either tribe, each had as
sumed that he belonged to the other, the enemy. He
had stuck close to Sanchez. That individual had actu
ally gotten off some effective shots with his crossbow
in the melee.

Only three horses remained.

"Horses are no problem," Heads Off assured the
lieutenant. "The Elk-dog men are rounding up loose
animals now."

It was a strange feeling to speak his own native
tongue once more. Even more strange was his fum
bling attempt to translate such terms as "elk-dog,"
now so important a part of his vocabulary.

"What is to be done now?"

Cabeza in his turn was having trouble in his rela

tionship to Heads Off. He had last seen the other as a cadet at the Academy, Upperclassman Juan Garcia. Now the same man was a painted chieftain, leader of a band of savages who appeared to be the finest squadron of lancers Cabeza had ever seen.

"Our camp is about two days east. We will carry the wounded on pole-drags."

There were, indeed, many riderless horses on the prairie that day. The men of the People were quickly gathering all they could. It was with great pride that the returning Bloods and Elk-dog warriors presented the best of the horses to the hair-faced lancers, the fighting men of their chief's father. The People had seen the valiant last-ditch stand from the ridge and had great respect for bravery.

They also shared their food supply. The Garcia party had lost everything in the flood. Campfires began to sparkle up and down the meadow as shadows grew long.

A number of saplings had been cut for pole-drags on which to transport the wounded. The likeliest horses were selected and tried, to have everything ready in the morning for departure.

South Wind, during all of this, was happily following Cabeza. She helped in the ministrations to the wounded, bandaging, carrying water, and, in general, endeared herself to the Garcia party. There was no doubt in anyone's mind, however, from the girl's entire attitude, that she belonged completely to Ramon Cabeza.

Sanchez for some time avoided the chief who had come to their rescue. Finally, Heads Off sought him out.

"Sanchez?"

"Yes, *señor*."

"You were with the Capitan's party when I was lost?"

"Yes, *señor*, we thought you dead."

Heads Off nodded. It seemed a lifetime ago. He hated to admit that he did not remember this strange little man, but there was nothing very memorable about him.

"It is no matter. I only wished to thank you. I am told it was you who brought my father to find me."

Sanchez could not speak with the lump that rose in his throat. He only smiled and nodded. A tear glistened in his eye.

He, Sanchez, was actually appreciated.

31
>> >> >>

Travel was slow and deliberate, with frequent stops to rest the wounded from the constant jolting of the pole-drags.

These conveyances, originally pulled by dogs, had been adapted to the horse in the last few seasons. There were always many lodge poles to transport when the nomadic buffalo hunters moved camp. These were effectively moved by crossing the ends of a pair of poles over the shoulders of an elk-dog. A rope or strip of skin around the animal's chest held the poles in position.

It had taken little imagination to see that objects could be tied to the dragging poles and soon it was commonplace to construct a platform on the poles behind the horse by lashing sticks across the two. Household supplies and possessions were transported in this way, as were small children and the elderly.

In this case, pole-drags transported the wounded. Great care had been taken to make them as comfortable as possible, but by nature of the device, it was a rough, jarring ride. The scouts in the lead constantly sought the most level route, bypassing the worst of the rocks and gullies.

Sometimes, however, there was no way around. Twice they encountered rough areas, easily crossed on foot or horseback, which were completely impassable with the drags. It was necessary to unload and carry the wounded men across, reassembling the conveyances on the other side.

Then at times came long stretches of easy traveling across the rolling prairie. The lush grasses, washed clean by the rain, were pleasant and sweet-smelling under the hooves of the travelers' horses. In the distance, they could see the scattered dark shapes of grazing buffalo or groups of lighter specks that were bands of antelope.

During one of these intervals, with Don Pedro Garcia resting fairly comfortably, Heads Off rode alongside Cabeza for a time. He found that he was hungry to hear his native tongue.

"Ramon, tell me about the Academy when you were last there. I did not finish, you know."

Cabeza chuckled. It was known that Cadet Juan Garcia had left the Academy quite suddenly after having been caught in an escapade with the Commandant's daughter.

"Yes, I remember. It was the talk of the Academy. We heard you were banished to New Spain."

The other nodded and smiled ruefully.

"That seems a very long time ago. I have a family now. Two sons! You must meet my wife. She is called Tall One."

His use of his native tongue was returning rapidly and he was enjoying the opportunity. Since he became Heads Off, warrior of the People, Juan had had no opportunity to share the tale of his adventures, except briefly with his wounded father. He recounted the frustrations of his repeated attempts to leave the People to return to his own kind.

Cabeza smiled sympathetically when the other told

of the broken lance point that had rendered him weaponless. He laughed outright when Juan related of his next attempt at departure, thwarted when he discovered that his mare was pregnant.

The lieutenant sobered rapidly, however, when he heard the story of the attack by the Head Splitters, who had obtained horses.

"You mean the People had none?"

"No, none at all! My mare was the first ever seen!"

He described the war party sent to recover from the enemy the kidnapped girls, one of whom was now his wife.

"And, it was after that, we were married. Then I knew I could not go back."

They rode in silence for a short while. Cabeza glanced at the slim girl riding beside him and South Wind smiled. He wondered if the wife of Juan Garcia could be as beautiful as this.

"Yes, my friend, I can understand how that might happen."

"But tell me of things at home."

The two visited, talking of mutual friends and acquaintances, of incidents at the Academy, of the instructors. Some were feared by the cadets, some respected, some revered. The young men discussed them all.

"Ramon, how did you happen to be on this expedition?"

"Your father hired me. Sanchez had talked him into a search for you. You really knew him before?"

Juan Garcia shook his head.

"I can't remember, but he must have been with the expedition. I'm told he led you here."

Cabeza shrugged.

"At least, we are here. There were times I was sure Sanchez had no idea where we were. Did you know he saved my life once?"

He recounted the story of that episode and Juan smiled.

"He seems an unlikely one for that, but men do strange things in battle."

Cabeza nodded.

"That is what your father said, before . . ."

He hated to mention Don Pedro's lapse into lunacy.

"Before what?"

"Before the last fight," he finished.

They stopped for the night near a clear stream. The camp was more relaxed and optimistic tonight, further from the scene of battle and the threat of the Head Splitters, should they decide to return.

Don Pedro, looking ashen pale after a grueling day of travel, was made comfortable on a pallet of robes. Everyone seemed concerned with his well-being and Cabeza finally realized that the wounded old warrior was being accorded the respect due the father of a chief.

After some rest and nourishment, the elder Garcia looked stronger.

"We reach my home tomorrow, father. Then you may meet your grandsons and their mother."

Juan Garcia was becoming continually more excited over that prospect.

Dusk fell and the stars winked awake, mirrored in the surface of the stream and in the points of light from the campfires. Cabeza prepared his robes for sleep and motioned to South Wind, preparing her own bed nearby.

"Come," he signed.

"No. It is not the way of my people."

She slipped into her own sleeping robes. Cabeza approached her bed, but met with firm resistance.

"No!"

Now he was completely confused. The girl had hardly left his side since the battle. Her every action said that she adored him and they had already spent one idyllic night in each other's arms. Now, for reasons he did not understand, he was being rebuffed.

"Why?" he signed.

"It is not our way!"

Feeling deprived, angry, and a little foolish, Cabeza sought his own robes, but found little sleep. Damn! The girl seemed so ready, so sensuous.

The previous right, he had not attempted to initiate any intimacy. The excitement of battle, the tenseness of exhaustion, the crowded proximity of the rest of the party, all contributed to an unlikely situation for romance.

But tonight, he had deliberately chosen a setting for their personal campfire that would be provocative. It was aloof from the others, screened for privacy by a fringe of dogwood along the creek. The view of the starlit stream and the distant prairie could not have been more beautiful.

And here he lay, fuming with frustrated anger in his blankets. Close beside him, but firmly wapped in her own robe, lay the girl. He was completely confused. At the earliest opportunity, he must ask Juan to explain this strange sequence of events.

32
» » »

Messengers had gone ahead to inform the People of the return of the war party. It would be a time of great feasting and celebration.

Immediately, Coyote and the others of the Bowstring Society began plans for the festivities. The victorious war party, with their guests from the faraway tribe of Heads Off, were expected by dark. Allowing one day for rest and preparation, the ceremonial dance and celebration was set for the following evening. That would allow time for the obtaining and preparation of food and the gathering of wood for the great fire which would in all probability last all night.

Tall One and her mother, Big Footed Woman, were busily trying to accomplish all the small details in preparation for the occasion. Never had they imagined that they would be able to entertain and honor the father of their beloved Heads Off. And, though they had learned that the older man was severely wounded, it was thought that he would be able to attend the dance in his honor.

The children, grandsons of the White Hair, were meticulously groomed and their hair was freshly braided with strips of otter skin. Little Owl, too young to know what was going on, submitted with the wide-eyed, solemn silence which had earned him his name. Eagle, nearly three summers now, was greatly enjoying the excitement of the occasion.

The youngsters were outfitted with the best of new garments and footwear and both women then turned attention to the preparation of gifts to be used in the warriors' dance. It would require a number of items to honor their men during the ceremony.

They had barely enough time to accomplish all these things. As the shadows from Sun Boy's torch began to lengthen, a watching youth came running from the top of the ridge.

"Here they come!"

The People poured forth to welcome the returning travelers, accompanied by a myriad of yapping dogs. Someone from the camp started the victory song and it was soon echoed by the first of the incoming warriors.

The Blood Society had painted their faces, a broad slash of crimson across the forehead. Other warriors wheeled and strutted and small groups made mock charges at an imaginary enemy.

Rejoicing in victory and pleased with the scarcity of casualties, the People swarmed over the returning war party, laughing and singing. There were many demonstrations of affection between wives and returned warriors. Men hoisted small children to ride before them in triumph on the horses' withers. Here and there a young wife swung up behind her husband on his horse to accompany him into the camp.

Though the formal feast and ceremonial would not be until the following day, there was no stopping the exuberance of the young people. Scarcely had everyone eaten when the drums were thumping their cadence and the dancing had begun.

For some, the revelry would last far into the night. For those of the Garcia party, exhaustion demanded rest. They were taken proudly into the lodges of new acquaintances among the war party of the People. It was an honor to have as a guest one of the warriors of the tribe of their chief.

Heads Off himself took his father and Ramon Cabeza into his lodge. Sanchez would stay in the adjacent dwelling, that of Coyote and Big Footed Woman.

The meeting of the elder Garcia with his son's family was a moment of great emotion for Heads Off. He and Cabeza had carried the old man into the lodge and settled him on a pallet of buffalo robes.

"Father, my wife."

Tall One nodded and smiled and the gallant old man took her hands.

"She is a woman of great beauty, my son. You have done well."

Self-consciously, the young man translated for his pleased and blushing wife, then turned to his small sons.

"Eagle, Little Owl, come and meet your grandfather."

Don Pedro Garcia, who had long believed his only son dead, now found himself with grandsons. The two youngsters came shyly forward, big-eyed and not understanding the importance of the occasion. Little Owl, barely big enough to toddle, was led forward by his mother.

Tears wet the cheeks of the old warrior as he laid a hand on the head of each in turn.

"They are fine, strong boys to be proud of, Juan. You tell their mother what I have said."

He sank back, exhausted, and was soon asleep. He did not even know when White Buffalo, the medicine man, came and examined the wound.

"I will make the strongest medicine I can, Heads Off. It is a bad wound. See, it steals his breath."

He indicated the rapid respiration of the sleeping man.

"It could allow his spirit to escape, too."

"Yes, uncle, I know."

Tall One now took charge of nursing the wounded Don Pedro. She was constantly at his side, ministering to his every want. Constantly, she offered him choice morsels to eat and sips of the freshest and coolest water. It seemed that she could not do enough to honor the father of her husband.

"Juan, your wife is as wonderful as she is beautiful."

It was next morning and Don Pedro was enjoying a sweet concoction of hackberries, pounded fine, mixed with buffalo fat and rolled into balls.

His son smiled.

"I know, father. I will tell her."

Tall One was pleased again. She was already becoming very fond of this dignified and gallant old man. She could see many of her husband's qualities in him.

White Buffalo, too, seemed to relate well to Don Pedro. Though they could not speak a word of each other's tongues, the two seemed to communicate well. They appeared to regard each other as contemporaries and mutual respect was evident.

Yet, with these personal relationships, it was generally accepted that the outlook for Don Pedro Garcia was not good. The People had seen many wounds of this type and understood the frustration of dealing with them. For the present, all that could be done was to keep the wounded man comfortable and attend to his wants. And, of course, to try to make the days which might be his last ones good days.

33

>> >> >>

Although the ceremonial dance was not to be held until dark, the entire day became one of celebration. There was an excitement in the air, a sense of expectation, a feeling that something was about to happen.

To the visitors, the mood was very like that of carnival time in their own land. There were contests of athletic skill, races both on foot and on horseback, and demonstrations of expertise with weapons.

The excitement was contagious. When a number of the Bloods challenged the Elk-dog Society to a contest with lances, the soldiers of the Garcia party were eager to observe.

Targets were set up. Hoops of green willow were placed up the hillside. Youngsters ran to tie the rings loosely to the scattered sumac bushes and the two competing groups readied for the run.

Two by two, the young warriors charged up the slope at an imaginary enemy. An Elk-dog warrior and one from the Blood Society would race out, thread a target ring on each lance point, and scuttle back to the starting line. There were wagers on each race, with constantly growing excitement.

Sergeant Perez of the lancer platoon approached Cabeza.

"Lieutenant, could we have permission to show them a frontal charge?"

"Well, why not?"

The lancers, though glad even to be alive, had felt a bit of chagrin over having been rescued by a group of savages. They needed an opportunity to demonstrate their own skill.

"I will ride with you," Cabeza finished impulsively.

There was a scurry to fetch weapons and equipment, to borrow horses, and the ragged half-strength platoon fell in at the base of the slope. Cabeza motioned to the youngsters to replace the willow hoop targets and ordered his platoon into line.

"We will show them a little close-order drill, then swing into a charge."

Even with horses unfamiliar with this sort of exercise, the lancers were impressive. They wheeled and turned, starting eight in line, splitting to a column of fours, then two abreast, circling and reforming.

By the time they had reversed the procedure, reforming into a single front to prepare for the charge, the warriors of the People were shouting encouragement.

"*Aiee!* Their elk-dog medicine is strong!"

The young men of the People were skilled enough as horsemen to recognize real ability when they saw it.

"Charge!"

As the eight-man front wheeled into position, Cabeza had spurred his horse in front of them to lead the charge up the slope. The horsemen surged upward, aiming weapons at targets of opportunity.

They crested the hill and wheeled, weapons held high, to ride loosely down the slope. Each lance had threaded its shaft with at least one willow hoop. Ca-

beza's sword held two of the rings and the weapon of
the sergeant displayed three. A roar of approval and
congratulation swelled from the horsemen of the
People.

Now the Bowstring Society took the opportunity to
show their skill. Targets of skins stuffed with dry
grass were carried up the slope. Youngsters arranged
the effigies among the bushes in lifelike partial
concealment.

Competition was keen and the skin targets were
moved further and further away. The number of warriors still in competition grew smaller, until at last
there were only two. At the final shot, a lucky puff of
wind caught the soaring projectile, deflecting it precisely into the center of the distant target. There was
a roar of laughter, along with cheers and congratu-
lations.

Someone suggested a demonstration with crossbows
and the crossbowmen gladly obliged. There were gasps
of amazement at the power and accuracy of the weapons. Especially at longer ranges, the short, heavy crossbow bolts made an impressive showing. On an impulse,
one of the Blood warriors raced up the hill to hang his
bullhide shield for a target. The flint-hard rawhide
was able to turn the point of any weapon known to
the People.

One bowman selected a steel-tipped bolt and in-
serted it carefully in the groove of his weapon. He
assumed the shooting stance and, with quick aim,
squeezed the lever. The missile twanged on its way.
In a moment, the shield jerked convulsively on the
bush and a murmur of amazed exclamation rose from
the nearest of the spectators.

"Aiee!"

"It has killed Yellow Hawk's shield!"

"The far-shoots bow has strong medicine."

Everyone clustered around to see the amazing oc-
currence. It was true. The bolt had actually penetrated
the hard rawhide of the shield. The point projected a
hand's span on the other side, with the shaft wedged
tightly in the defect.

Instantly, crossbowmen increased tremendously in prestige, as the strength of their medicine was realized. Those lodges now entertaining crossbowmen basked in reflected glory. Sanchez strutted pompously.

Further demonstration, however, was precluded by the scarcity of crossbow bolts. The skirmishes and the final battle had used nearly the entire supply carried by the expedition and few were recoverable. Those left were to be hoarded carefully.

As shadows grew longer, the impromptu activities dwindled. The People returned to their lodges to dress and ready themselves for the celebration. By the time Sun Boy's torch had disappeared, light from the fire was replacing its illumination. Several older warriors gathered around the dance drum and, softly, tentative thumping of the dogwood sticks on the big skin drumhead began.

The People came by twos and threes and family groups, drifting toward the dance arena. Each was wearing his best finery, garments of soft-tanned skins with intricate decorations of quillwork.

Members of the Bowstring Society arrived with the dignity befitting their years and station in life. Most were near middle age or older, their warrior careers dating from the days before the elk-dog. An occasional younger man joined them. The use of the traditional methods was by choice for these. All youngsters in the Rabbit Society were instructed in athletic skills and the use of weapons and horses. Some simply chose the role of the warrior on foot, using the time-honored bow and arrows. They were inducted into the Bowstring Society when they achieved warrior status. Their dress and ceremonial face paint was that of ancient tribal custom.

The Bowstrings, with their ties to tradition, were charged with the planning and execution of the celebration. Older Bowstring warriors, unable to physically participate in the dance, would beat the cadence on the great drum and chant the traditional songs of valor.

Next came the men of the Elk-dog Society, the younger warrior group. They arrived with their young families, dressed and painted as befitted the station of rising warriors in the tribe. These were the horsemen, the new warrior generation, proven but still rising in wealth and influence in the tribe. Their facial paint had been modified in design, especially in the narrow yellow stripes and dots across the cheekbones. Yet the influence of tradition could be easily seen.

The Elk-dogs stood, visiting easily with their families and with the Bowstrings. Heads Off himself arrived, wearing around his neck on a thong the silvery horse bit that had now assumed the status of a talisman. It had become almost a sacred symbol of the acquisition of the horse, the powerful elk-dog medicine of the People.

Warriors carefully lifted Don Pedro Garcia and carried him to the celebration. The old man was made comfortable on a pallet of soft robes, with a willow back rest to support him in a semireclining position. Near him were the other wounded, now gaining strength in their recovery. These, two from the Garcia party and one from the People, would be honored heroes in the dance celebration.

Still, there was an air of waiting. The People kept peering expectantly toward the darkening perimeter of the camp. At last someone pointed.

"*Aiee*, here they come!"

The Blood Society, arrogant nonconformists, were arriving in a group. These were the young rebels, so recently reaccepted by the tribe. Their dress was flamboyant, their facial paint stark and challenging. The broad crimson band across the forehead was accentuated by a wide black horizontal stripe under each eye. Decorations on their capes and bodies were uniformly red and black. With their proud bearing, the advancing group made a spectacular picture as they approached the fire. Their leader, Red Dog, nodded pleasantly to the older men of the Bowstring Society and the group stood waiting.

White Buffalo stepped forward, arms upraised. He held a tortoise-shell rattle in one hand, in the other one of the small, shapeless medicine bags of his profession.

"Let the dance begin!"

34
>> >> >>

Cabeza and his everpresent companion, South Wind, found seats next to the arena, near the young chief of the People. This man, to Ramon Cabeza, was still Juan Garcia, his boyhood acquaintance from home. The lieutenant was unaware or perhaps unwilling to acknowledge the tremendous sense of security that Heads Off represented. He was the only person among the People with whom Cabeza could fully communicate.

To enter into a ceremony one has never seen is a worrisome thing. He knew that the members of his party would be expected to participate to some extent, but beyond that he was unsure. He desperately needed someone who would be able to inform him what was going on.

South Wind was very helpful, but their conversation was necessarily limited by the nature of the sign language. A general idea was no problem, but the intricacies of the meaning and symbolism of the ceremonies were beyond such simple signals. Cabeza was anxious that he might not respond correctly and at the proper time.

Apparently Heads Off, formerly Juan Garcia, sensed his guest's distress.

"I will explain what is happening, Ramon," he assured Cabeza in their boyhood tongue.

The young chief himself could well remember the first dance celebration he had observed. It had been only a few seasons ago. He now marveled that he had seen no significance in the ceremony. He remembered that, to an outsider, the entire affair would be only a boring repetition of chanted nonsense syllables and endless gyrations of painted bodies.

"First, there will be a procession, led by the Bowstrings. They circle the area, announcing the ceremony. Then there is a dance for the warriors, before the story songs begin. Don't worry—I will tell you as we go. For now, you stay here."

Heads Off rose to join the other warriors and South Wind cuddled reassuringly against Cabeza, her hand resting gently on his arm.

The procession was led by White Buffalo and two of the oldest warriors of the Bowstrings. One, thought Cabeza, seemed barely able to totter around the circular arena. Methodically, they wound their way around the periphery of the circle, followed by the other warriors. All were singing in cadence to the thump of the great drum—and hair prickled on the back of Cabeza's neck. There was a deep stirring of primitive rhythms in forgotten recesses of his very soul. He found himself swaying and moving with the others, in time with the beats of the chant.

Close behind the Bowstrings came the warriors of the Elk-dog Society, proudly stepping, swaying, and singing. Then came the Bloods, spectacular in the dress and paint, lusty in their rendering of the traditional songs.

Three times the parade circled the arena and then the drums stopped. The dancers scattered for a moment, returning to their respective families for minor adjustments to their paint and finery.

Soon, however, the circle began to reform and the drum started again. This time, the rhythm was slightly different. The dancers, likewise, faced toward the center of the circle and began to step in time to the drumbeats. The step was sideways now, everyone moving to the left in a clockwise rotation. Cabeza noted that among the warriors, women now joined the circle, stepping and gliding.

The medicine man now stepped to the center of the circle and loudly made an announcement of some sort. A few seated warriors rose self-consciously from their scattered places and joined the shifting circle.

The medicine man repeated his call, looking directly at Cabeza and the others of the Garcia party scattered behind him. Confused, the lieutenant turned to the girl beside him.

"What does he say?"

"He asks other warriors to join the Warrior Dance."

He still did not understand. What in Christ's name was he supposed to do? He glanced around in a momentary panic. His lancers sat behind him, also puzzled, but not quite so concerned. They looked to him for leadership.

Heads Off danced past them, now accompanied by his tall, attractive wife. They both smiled at the visitors' confusion.

"Come on, Ramon," the chief called. "Bring your lancers!"

Cabeza struggled to his feet and motioned to his companions. The group began to find places in the circle and, impulsively, Cabeza reached a hand to South Wind. He pulled her forward with him, crowding into place just to the right of Heads Off and Tall One. The girl's eyes sparkled with excitement.

"This is the visitors' dance," the young chief spoke above the thump of the drum. "Any visiting warrior is invited to join in. There are three from our Northern band, one from the Mountain band. Even a couple of the Growers are here. And your party, of course."

The circle moved slowly to the left, with the monotonous chant now moving steadily. Cabeza found the rhythm not difficult, and soon was stepping with growing confidence. He glanced at the girl beside him. She flashed a bright smile and such an adoring look that he felt like the mightiest warrior alive. He heard a pleased, lilting trickle of laughter at his other elbow and turned to smile at his host's wife. Tall One nodded approvingly.

The visitors' dance ended and people resumed their seats. Other dances followed. One for the women only, one by each of the warrior societies. Children of the Rabbit Society performed one dance, hopping enthusiastically around the arena to the amusement of proud parents. It was apparent to the visitors that the People regarded their children with the utmost importance.

Finally, the dance proper began. Heads Off was now seated beside Cabeza and able to more fully explain the sequence of events.

"Now there will be songs of warriors. The first songs tell of battles a long time ago, famous deeds by heroes of the People. The dancers will act out the stories. Then the songs come close to the present and the last ones will be about the fight at the flooded creek."

With this explanation, Cabeza could thoroughly enjoy the dances. Occasionally, he asked a question of his host or conversationally exchanged a series of hand signs with the girl beside him.

There were interminable songs and dances. Sometimes Heads Off would explain in detail.

"This is the story of the Great Battle with the Head Splitters. It happened after we got the horses."

Finally, there was a ballad which seemed to depict almost current happenings. People turned to look at the visitors, as a group of dancers slowly retreated backward across the arena.

South Wind tugged at Cabeza's sleeve.

"That is you, Ramon," she signed.

Heads Off turned.

"Yes, that is your defense at the creek. It is strong medicine among the People that your handful of lancers held off the Head Splitters."

South Wind smiled adoringly and proudly squeezed Cabeza's arm.

"Oh yes, Ramon," the young chief spoke casually, "there is one other thing. When you asked the girl to join you in the warriors' dance, that was a proposal of marriage."

35

>> >> >>

It was nearly noon of the following day before Cabeza managed to seek out the young chief for a serious conversation.

"Juan, I have to talk with you. Can we be alone?"

The other nodded. He had some idea where this talk would lead.

"Of course. Let us walk."

The two men strolled out of the village, responding occasionally to pleasant greetings by various members of the People. The chief indicated the direction and they casually ascended a nearby hill. Juan Garcia seated himself on a boulder and pointed to another nearby.

"I come here sometimes to think. Did you ever see anything like this, Ramon?"

He traced the horizon with a sweeping gesture. Cabeza followed his gaze, again impressed by the vastness of the place. Range followed range of the low rolling hills, clothed in the lush grasses of the prairie. In the distance, the green became blue, until at last it was impossible to discern between the blue of the furthest inundations of the plains and the blue of the azure sky.

Buffalo dotted the distant meadows and fluffy white clouds sent blue circles of shadow gliding across the green expanse. Nearer their hilltop, an eagle swept past on fixed wings, uttering her high-pitched cry. Nearer at hand, a red-winged grasshopper clattered into the air and fluttered to rest a few steps away, becoming instantly invisible again as soon as it became motionless.

"Yes, Ramon, you wished to talk?"

Cabeza, startled, came back from his reverie with some embarrassment.

"What? Oh yes."

Where should he begin?

"It is about the girl?" the other encouraged.

Cabeza nodded.

"Yes, that is part of it. I have to make some decisions."

The man in breechclout and moccasins waited, silent. He had, he knew, undergone much the same sort of soul-searching himself not too many summers past.

"How can I start? First, I know my responsibility is to your father. I am paid to lead the expedition's fighting men. Now . . ." he shrugged. "I will have to lead the entire party home, what remains of it. There is Sanchez, of course, but you know . . ."

The other nodded, waiting.

"And how long until your father, *Señor* Garcia, is able to travel?"

He heaved a deep sigh.

"Then the girl. You say I have to marry her?"

"Don't you want to?"

"Of course. But, my God, man, I can't stay here with her. I have to take the expedition home. And I might never be able to return."

Juan Garcia's respect for this young man had been steadily growing. His loyalty and dependability were apparently above reproach. The elder Garcia had chosen his man well. Now, yet another facet of the lieutenant's makeup was seen. The average man would think very lightly of a temporary liaison with a native girl. One could go through the motions of whatever mumbo jumbo was required. Then, when it became convenient, the girl could be abandoned with impunity.

Hence, Heads Off had been a trifle uneasy about this relationship. He felt protective over the girl and defensive toward any threat to her well-being. South Wind was, after all, one of the People, to be defended from men of other tribes. And marriage customs of the People were very strict. He smiled inwardly at the thought that he now regarded his fellow cadet from the Academy as an outsider. His own affinity for the People still astonished him.

"Cabeza, you could marry her—and then just leave her here when you go."

For a moment, he thought the lieutenant was ready to strike him. Anger and disbelief distorted Cabeza's face.

"Mother of God, Garcia! Could you abandon your wife and sons?"

That was the reaction the other had been seeking. Inwardly, he nodded approval. Outwardly, he waved aside the protests of the other.

"Of course not, Ramon. I only wondered how you felt. I have been through the same problem, you know."

He pondered in silence a moment.

"You really love this girl, don't you, Ramon?"

It was more a statement than a question.

"My friend," answered Cabeza, "I can understand why you were never able to go back to Spain. But I must."

The other nodded sympathetically.

"It strikes me, Ramon, that South Wind would follow you to the ends of the earth."

"You mean—take her *back* with me?"

"Would you be embarrassed by her?"

For a moment, Cabeza became indignant again. Then, relaxed.

Juan, I would be proud to take her anywhere as my wife."

His comparion was pleased.

"And so you should be. She is not only beautiful, but a woman of great courage."

He paused a long moment.

"For me, it was wrong to think of going back to Spain. For you, it may be right. Now, it will be some time before Don Pedro is able to travel. Why not marry the girl and be happy while you wait?"

"How is this done?"

"The ceremony is simple. Her father just spreads a robe over the shoulders of the couple in a public announcement. But first, you have to give him something of value."

"You mean, *buy* her?"

"No no, you just honor her family with a gift."

Cabeza shrugged, dejected.

"But I have nothing!"

He picked idly at the sleeve of his threadbare shirt, as if to indicate that it was all he owned.

"He will know that, Ramon. But it should show some sacrifice on your part. Why not give him your horse?"

Cabeza's face reflected consternation. He had commandeered one of the Garcia stallions after the death of his own animal. To lose it now would put him on foot again.

"But, Juan, I *need* my horse!"

"A horse is no problem. I will give you all the horses you want. But the gift to her father must be *your* horse."

"And how is this thing done?"

"You lead the horse through the camp and tie it in front of her father's lodge. Then when he comes out, ask him for his daughter. You can use the sign talk."

"Suppose he refuses?"

"He will not refuse. It will be a great honor for him to have such a warrior as you in his family."

"But Juan, where would we go? I can't bring a bride home to your lodge!"

Heads Off laughed.

"You'll find this hard to believe, my friend. Most of

the young couples move in with the girl's family until they can afford their own lodge. It makes mighty hunters of the young men, trying to save enough skins for a lodge cover. The girls become pretty proficient at tanning, too."

Cabeza looked crestfallen.

"There is another possibility, Ramon. The weather is good at this time. The two of you can go off by yourselves for a few days. The People often live in a brush arbor in summer or when they're traveling and don't want to put up the big lodge. South Wind will know how to build one."

36
>> >> >>

The idea of a few days alone with South Wind in the beauty of nature was a very appealing thought for Cabeza. That very evening, he led the gray stallion proudly through the village and stopped in front of the lodge. The father of South Wind emerged from the doorway, ostensibly to see what was going on, though by this time he knew full well.

"*Ah-koh*, uncle, I would ask for your daughter, South Wind."

Cabeza had been carefully instructed in proper etiquette.

Lame Fox hesitated a long time, as was proper.

"What will you give?"

"My best elk-dog."

My only elk-dog, in fact, he thought miserably. What if he refuses?

The warrior appeared to consider long, then finally spoke.

"Come in. We will talk."

The invitation into the lodge was equivalent to ac-

172

ceptance and Cabeza relaxed. The host held the door skin aside and they entered the dim of the lodge.

Lame Fox indicated a pile of robes for the guest to sit.

South Wind sat beside her mother on the opposite side of the lodge. Her eyes sparkled with excitement. Cabeza wondered if he could manage the sign talk well enough to handle this situation. Well, if it became too difficult, perhaps he could induce Heads Off to come and speak for him. He heaved a deep sigh.

"The weather has been very good," he began.

The faces across the fire broke into friendly smiles. It was a situation of great honor to have the war chief of the Hairfaces marry into one's family.

"Yes," signed Lame Fox. "Very good."

Preparations were soon under way for the nuptial ceremony of the daughter of Lame Fox. She would be given in marriage to the war chief of the Hairfaces, the tribe of the great chief of the People, Heads Off.

Lame Fox was extremely pleased. As one of the Bowstring Society, he had little use for the great gray elk-dog given by his prospective son-in-law. Still, the prestige of owning such a fine animal was important. There were few families among the People who could boast such a possession. And the family of Lame Fox had never been wealthy. An injury in his youth had resulted in a pronounced limp. It made it difficult for him to achieve great success at the hunt.

True, he had managed to keep his children fed and a lodge over their heads, but it had been hard. Even now, as he began to feel the gnawing bite of Cold Maker in his stiff knee on chilly mornings, he wondered what the future held. He had begun to understudy the work of Stone Breaker, maker of weapons, against the time he could no longer hunt. His work was not yet proficient enough for prestige and recognition, but now the People would at least know the name of Lame Fox, whose daughter had married well.

And the daughter! *Aiee,* she had been a problem. Headstrong and unpredictable, the girl seemed to take after the family of her mother, Chickadee. They were of the Eastern band of the People, noted for foolishness and poor judgment.

Ah well, theirs had been an exciting marriage. Even with the extra concern over the volatile South Wind and her childhood escapades, it had been good. Chickadee was a good wife.

True, Lame Fox had sometimes wondered if this, their oldest child, would ever marry. She had spurned the attentions of all the young men. This secretly pleased her father, who saw none worthy of South Wind anyway. All the young men of the Rabbit Society as she grew up had been defeated by her in running, swimming, or in the proficient use of weapons. Lame Fox had wondered if there might be any warrior among the People who would be a fit partner for his fiery daughter.

When she had been abducted, he and her mother had despaired of ever seeing her again. Now, in the space of a few short days, events had occurred so rapidly that Lame Fox could hardly comprehend.

Here was his returned daughter, more mature and more attractive than ever. Circumstances had placed her in a situation to become practically a heroine of the People. In addition, it required no imagination to see that her medicine with the young hair-face chief was very strong. Lame Fox was proud.

Now it remained only to set a time for the ceremony and make certain there would be enough food for the feast. Lame Fox, Chickadee, and South Wind were discussing the matter in front of their lodge.

"Spotted Cat owes me meat. I will ask him."

"Yes, my husband. Deer Woman will help me cook. Probably Tall One and Big Footed Woman, also."

"Father, when will the ceremony be?"

Lame Fox shrugged.

"When can you be ready, Chickadee?"

The bright eyes of the little woman danced and Lame Fox thought once more how easy it was to see how she had come by her name.

"Would two suns be soon enough?"

"For me, yes," answered Lame Fox solemnly. "For South Wind, I am not sure."

He smiled at his daughter.

"Two suns will be good, father. It will give us time to find a place to be together."

South Wind already had a place in mind. Upstream from the village, not quite half a sun's journey, was a hidden canyon she had discovered as a child. The People had camped nearby for a season and South Wind had used the retreat for all the pretending of a small girl. It was protected on three sides by steep, rocky walls and a sparkling spring fed the tiny stream that wandered among the rocks and trees.

South Wind was dreamily planning the bower that she and Rah-mone would build together for their first temporary home.

"Look!"

Her mother interrupted her reverie.

"Coyote comes!"

Even from a distance, it was apparent that something was wrong. Something in the slope of the little man's shoulders, the downward tilt of his head, sent the information ahead of him. Anxiously, the family of Lame Fox watched as Coyote came closer.

"*Ah-koh*, my friend," greeted Lame Fox.

Coyote stood a long moment.

"*Ah-koh*, Lame Fox. I have bad news."

Thoughts of trouble raced through the minds of the others. Had Rah-mone changed his mind? Had something happened to him? South Wind leaped to her feet.

"No no," Coyote shook his head, "it is only that the marriage must be postponed."

The others relaxed slightly, but stood waiting, still concerned.

"The chief's father is dying."

37

>> >> >>

Don Pedro Garcia had appeared to do so well initially that news of his worsening condition came as a shock to many. Daily activities continued, but there was a sort of hushed reverence around the lodge of the chief's family.

People shook their heads and told one another that they had thought so. It is a rare thing to recover from such a chest wound.

The more philosophic of the People talked of how it was good that the old hair-face chief had been able to enjoy his son's adopted people for a time.

In truth, it had meant more to Don Pedro Garcia than anyone could ever know. In a certain sense, his dreams for his only son were being fulfilled and he, Don Pedro, was privileged to see it.

He had thought of his son as a leader of men and, as all could see, this had been accomplished. It was in a strange way in a strange land, but all the same, Juan Garcia had become a leader.

Likewise, it was very important to the old man that his son was respected. There was no questioning the looks of admiration among the younger men of the tribe.

Then there was the family of his son. Again, it came in a strange land, but Don Pedro appreciated the opportunity to know them. Though he could speak or understand scarcely a word of his daughter-in-law's tongue, he had come to love her. He admired her beauty, her quick smile, her gentle touch. Ah yes, he could not better have chosen the mother of his grandsons had he picked her himself.

The boys were the idols of his waking hours. Don Pedro watched them endlessly. They would be too small to remember ever having seen their grandfather, but he felt that he could die happily, having seen the next generation, the offspring of his loins. What stalwart boys! The older, Eagle, he was called, was aggressive, athletic, and well liked. His ready smile would take him far.

The younger child, Owl, was quiet, almost timid. He was introspective and thoughtful. The huge dark eyes of his mother peered cautiously from the infant's face, seeming to understand all things. Ah yes, this one! This one is the dreamer, thought Don Pedro. He will make a great thinker.

The old man's major regret was that his wife, *Doña* Isabal, would not be able to see her grandchildren.

"Cabeza, you must tell my wife of all these things when you return."

"No, *Señor*, you will tell her yourself."

"Thank you, Ramon, but I know. You forget, I am an old soldier. I have seen chest wounds."

He paused to cough, the exhausting hack that was becoming worse. Cabeza shuddered at the sound.

"You tell her," Garcia finished weakly, sinking back on the pallet.

It was only the next day that the old man became unconscious and the word rippled through the Elk-dog band. The old chief, father of Heads Off, was dying.

Yet three more days the old warrior fought. The
People were amazed at his stamina, though failing to
understand his reluctance to cross over into the Spirit
World. To them it would have been a natural progres-
sion. In the words of their Death Song,

The grass and the sky go on forever,
But today is a good day to die!

For the People, any day was "a good day to die"
when the sequence of events decreed it. So there was
puzzlement at the old hair-face's stubborn refusal to
let go, even as it drew admiration.

White Buffalo was almost constantly present, chant-
ing, dancing, sprinkling pungent herbs on the hot coals
of the fire to fill the lodge with fragramt smoke. The
medicine man used every technique and ceremony in
his knowledge to assist in the comfortable passing of
the spirit.

Comatose and unable to take nourishment, Don
Pedro grew weaker, his breathing more shallow, until
at last, in the dark of a cloudy, drizzly night, the breathing stopped. His son, who had been at his side almost
constantly, was dozing, half asleep. At the cessation
of the rhythmic quiet sound of breathing, Heads Off
came suddenly awake. The big dark eyes of Tall One
looked deeply into his.

"His spirit has crossed over, my husband."

Immediately, her clear voice rose in the Mourning
Song. It was picked up and echoed in the adjacent
lodge of Coyote, then by another and another, as the
People came awake to mourn the loss of their chief's
father. The song would usher in the period of mourning, carried out over the next three days.

Now Heads Off was faced with a dilemma. The
People were already preparing to carry out the traditional ceremonies of burial. The body would be placed
on an elevated funeral scaffold after the customs of
the tribe.

Juan Garcia had been raised in the Church, though
he had never taken the teachings very seriously. Now

somehow, he wondered if he should not insist on a Christian burial, with interment in the ground. There were problems, of course. There was no priest to officiate, none among the party, even, who knew the proper procedure.

There were even more basic problems. How was one to dig a grave? The People had no tools for digging in the earth. The young man sought out his father-in-law, his friend, adviser, and confidant.

"Coyote, I am troubled. How can I be sure I am doing the right thing? Should my father be buried with the customs of his own tribe or that of the People?"

The pudgy little man was quiet a long while, drawing slowly on his pipe. His eyes were half closed in thought, and once the younger man thought he had gone to sleep. At last he spoke.

"My son, there are many paths to the top of the hill, but all reach the same spot." He spread his hands in an exaggerated shrug.

"What does it matter? Your father has crossed over on our path and may continue it to the top. But I know his people have their own medicine. I would see no harm in using both. Either way, he is a chief, and will be a chief in the Spirit World."

It was a long speech for Coyote, but Heads Off found it somehow very comforting.

Don Pedro Garcia received the honor of a chief of the People. He would depart this world with his weapons, food for the journey, and dressed for battle, befitting a warrior. His armor had been lost in the flood, but the great sword was placed beside him as the body was wrapped for the scaffold.

There was some discussion as to whether the sword should be broken to release the spirit. Some tribes known to the People believed that every item involved must be so treated. Heads Off assured them that in the tribe of his father this was not necessary.

Likewise, there was discussion of his need for a horse to ride in the Spirit World. Should an elk-dog be killed beneath the scaffold to furnish transportation on the other side? Again, Heads Off advised against it

"In his Spirit World, there will be elk-dogs," he assured.

"*Aiee!*" Coyote answered. "His is a strong medicine!"

The ceremony at the funeral scaffold was brief. The procession wound its way to the site, to the chant of the Mourning Song, and the carefully wrapped body was placed upon it. The choice bits of food, a skin of water, and the old warrior's weapon were arranged to be convenient to him. The song became quiet.

For want of a better idea, Perez, the sergeant of lancers, recited a Hail Mary while the People stood quietly in respect for the Hairfaces' medicine.

In contrast, or perhaps in support, White Buffalo chanted the corresponding ceremonial ritual of the People. Thus, in this strange mixture of cultures, was the old warrior honored as he was ushered from this world to the next.

Coyote voiced the feelings of the group as they turned away to return to the village.

"My friends, we have seen the passing of a chief."

38
>> >> >>

Ramon Cabeza lay on the soft fur of a buffalo robe and felt the warmth of sunshine on his bare chest. He turned to look at the girl beside him and found that she was awake also, her large dark eyes watching him quietly.

It had been three days now since their marriage. Lame Fox had proudly spread the robe around the shoulders of the couple and they had walked from the village together to spend a few days in solitude.

Time was short. Already it was the Moon of Ripening and on some mornings there was a sharp chill in the air. It would be necessary for the expedition to depart shortly, to complete the journey south before the onslaught of Cold Maker.

Cabeza had discussed the possibility of wintering among the People, but Heads Off advised against it. If there were any delay after the coming of spring, any unforeseen circumstance, they might easily miss the return of the ship.

"I would be pleased and proud to have you stay, Ramon, but there is much risk. If you fail to show up at the appointed time, your ship's captain will sail on and report you lost."

So it had been decided. Cabeza and South Wind would proceed with their marriage and their brief sojourn for privacy. Meanwhile, Heads Off, Sanchez, and Sergeant Perez would see to the gathering of supplies and equipment for the journey.

The visitors would be escorted through the country of the Head Splitters, even as far as the hair-face camp that Cabeza spoke of. Long Elk would lead a party of warriors as an honor guard, proven men of the Elk-dog Society.

These preparations could easily proceed during the temporary absence of Cabeza and his bride. Then the group would depart before the Moon of Falling Leaves. The Elk-dog men, traveling rapidly, could return to meet the People for winter camp in the southern part of their territory.

Meanwhile, the party under Cabeza would winter with the garrison at the river or perhaps with Lizard's people in the Caddo country. Then they would easily be able to meet the galleon at the appointed time for the sea voyage home. For the first time in a long while, things seemed to be falling into place.

Cabeza and South Wind had spent three idyllic days alone together. They were like delighted children, learning words and phrases of each other's language.

South Wind had many things to show her new husband. She led him to all the hidden corners of the rocky glen where she had played as a child. They watched silvery minnows in the quiet stretches of the stream or swam together in a beaver pool just below their campsite.

They would emerge from the water and lie naked on the robe in the mottled sunshine under a great sycamore, allowing the warm rays to dry crystal droplets on their skin. They watched fluffy clouds drift over their little paradise and, in the sign language tried to describe what shapes of animals, birds, and trees they resembled.

A pair of quail and their half-grown brood inhabited the canyon and many times they saw the graceful birds slipping quietly through the undergrowth. South Wind puckered her lips in the whistling challenge call of the male bird. Much to Cabeza's amusement, the cock quail, bristling with indignation, strutted up almost to the edge of their robe, ready to fight the unseen intruder.

Cabeza had never before been in a situation where there were endless hours to merely sit and watch and wonder at the world around him. They watched, unmoving, as a doe and her mottled fawn stepped carefully down to drink at the beaver pool. At another time they might be hunted for food, but for now, with supplies in plenty, the graceful animals were merely fellow inhabitants of the glen.

Best of all were the times when the young couple merely spent quiet hours in each other's arms. They made love in the warmth of the day's sunshine and bundled in the warm furry robes of their bed, cuddling close against the night's chill. Cabeza, at these times, would have liked to forget for all eternity the responsibilities of the outside world and relax here in the security of their private little paradise forever.

They were at the beaver pond on the afternoon when their ecstasy was shattered. Both had just emerged from the water and they had run, laughing, to the waiting robe under the sycamore. They were sitting, facing each other, and playfully flicking droplets of water from each other's skin. These episodes had come to signal for both the preliminaries to a warm, prolonged embrace.

Cabeza was relishing the look of adoration in the girl's eyes as she teasingly touched him lightly across the chest and stomach. He was becoming aroused and was on the verge of playfully grabbing the teaser in a mock-ferocious bear hug for a rolling tussle on the robe.

Suddenly, the smiling, teasing expression on the pretty face changed to one of utter horror. South Wind had been gazing full in his face, but now lifted her eyes ever so slightly to look past him to something beyond.

Fighting to overcome his complete preoccupation, Cabeza whirled and rolled, instinctively dodging whatever danger was reflected in the terror-stricken eyes of South Wind. Almost at the same time, he heard the muffled clop of a horse's hoof. There, only a few paces away, sat Lean Bull on an efficient-looking war-horse.

There was an expression of complete triumph on the painted face. They were caught in the open, with nowhere to run for defense. Both were naked and their weapons were back at the brush arbor near their fire. Even at the time, Cabeza felt a flash of burning resentment that the man had probably been observing them for days, watching for the right moment.

Cabeza considered briefly the possibility of sprinting across the meadow to his weapons. Even on foot, the lance would serve well. He quickly abandoned the thought. Before he had gone a few steps, the horse would be upon him, its rider swinging the deadly club.

He glanced at the beaver pool. Could they throw themselves into the water and swim the few strokes to the other side? No, there was no escape there. The horse could easily follow and on the other side was a steep rocky face, impossible to climb.

Lean Bull chuckled and Cabeza realized that the intruder had already evaluated all of these possibilities. Even as this thought occurred to him, Lean Bull began the swinging arc with his heavy war club, gaining with each circling motion the momentum that could deliver a crushing death blow.

The defenseless pair scrambled to their feet. Cabeza gave South Wind a shove toward the pool.

"Quick! In the water!"

He did not know whether the girl would understand him, but this was the only possibility he saw, even though temporary. The attacker was principally inter-

ested in the destruction of Cabeza. Maybe he could
delay the onslaught long enough for the girl to escape.
If she swam to the head of the pool, there might be
shelter among the rocks.

Lean Bull dug heels into the horse's flanks and the
animal leaped forward in a deadly rush. Cabeza waited
and, at the last possible moment, jumped behind the
bole of the sycamore. The whirling club crashed against
the bark, sending shattered splinters flying. A patch of
denuded trunk the size of one's palm glistened white
in the mottled sunlight.

The horseman wheeled to strike again and Cabeza
dodged, keeping the bulk of the tree between them.
The horse was quick, however, expertly anticipating
and dodging to block the escape of the man on foot.
To the experienced animal, this was not much different than following the dodging course of a buffalo's
attempted escape.

For a moment, there was a stalemate. As long as
Cabeza remained at the tree, the whirling club could
not reach him. Unfortunately, neither could he escape. The standoff must end in either of two ways.
The quarry must break and run, to be cut down from
behind, or he must eventually tire and fail to continue
the quick footwork that now kept him from destruction. Lean Bull smiled with anticipation.

Both men reckoned without South Wind. The girl
was frantically looking for anything to use as a weapon.
A rock, a stick, anything to help her husband. She
scrambled along the shore, searching. On this side of
the pool were only small white gravelly stones, not
big enough to throw. Likewise, there were no trees or
underbrush on this side. Nothing, except the big lone
sycamore.

Frantically, she ran stumbling along the bank toward
the beaver dam. There, the animals had been cutting
small cottonwoods. Bright new yellow sticks woven
into the dam contrasted with the dark gray-brown
of the older materials. Her eye fell on a discarded
length of sapling, nearly as long as her arm and

as thick as a man's wrist. She seized the object and hurried back.

South Wind, during her days in the Rabbit Society, had delighted in her athletic ability. Too slight of build to compete with her male counterparts at wrestling, she had determined to excel in running and in the use of weapons. Her skill with the throwing sticks had been unsurpassed for several seasons. Many a rabbit had found its way to the lodge of Lame Fox during this time.

Now she sprinted back toward the tree, hefting the balance of the cottonwood stick. It would do. It must.

The girl panted to a stop, unheeded for the moment by either man. She circled, waiting for the right moment. The throw must be true. There could be but one.

Cabeza feinted left and dodged right, but the skilled buffalo horse anticipated and was there before him. This move, however, brought the horse and rider out from behind the tree.

The yellow cottonwood beaver-cutting arched gracefully end over end through the air, with all the force and accuracy of South Wind's expertise. Lean Bull caught only a glimpse of some flying object before it struck, just in front of the left ear. Limply he slid from the horse and landed heavily on his side. The animal bolted away and Lean Bull struggled to rise, breathless, confused and uncertain. Instantly, he was bowled over by the rush of two naked bodies.

Cabeza grasped the shaft of the stone war club at each end and pressed it against the warrior's throat, choking him against the ground. South Wind was snatching at the thong of the man's breechclout, searching for the knife she knew he kept there. Her hand encountered the hilt and she ripped the weapon from its sheath. In one sweeping motion, the razor-sharp flint swung in a precise arc and buried itself in the soft underbelly of the struggling warrior.

The struggles quieted and the two victors, breathless, sat back on their heels to look at each other in disbelief. Cabeza was breathing heavily, ragged gasps that showed how near exhaustion he had been. He rose and staggered over to fall on the rumpled buffalo robe. South Wind ran to fall on her knees beside him and the young man appreciatively circled her with an arm.

Once again, the girl had saved his life.

39

>> >> >>

One more night the young couple spent in their retreat. It had been late afternoon by the time the attack of Lean Bull took place, too late to do anything but prepare for the night.

The episode had brought them even closer together, but for them, the magic of their secret glen had been destroyed. It could never be the same for them after the presence of the intruder. Both knew, by the time they arose, that the day had come to return to the People.

The preparations for departure took somewhat longer than necessary. Both young people were reluctant to leave. There seemed the vague hope that somehow the event of the previous afternoon would prove not to have happened. But it was not to be. The presence of the enemy warrior's horse, tethered and grazing in the little meadow, was a reminder.

They made a small pack of their remaining food and rolled their sleeping robes for traveling. They had walked in, to avoid the inconvenience of caring for horses. Now they chose to walk on their return, allowing the horse to carry their possessions.

Sun Boy was just past the top of his daily run when they approached the village. Children ran ahead with news of their return and that the couple had somehow acquired an elk-dog!

There were many exclamations of surprise as the story of Lean Bull's attack was related.

"He must have watched us for days," Cabeza confided to Heads Off.

"Yes, I had forgotten that he vowed vengeance at the creek. That was careless of me, Ramon!"

"My friend, I am the careless one! We were very lucky!"

It had been decided during the absence of the newlyweds that the entire band would move, to travel with the visitors for a time toward the winter camp. A site had been chosen to the southeast, one of perennial appeal to the People. It was of value not only for its sheltered location, but for its great beauty. For many winters, this had been one of the favorite places for the Elk-dog band and they returned every few seasons.

Word of the move passed through the band. It would be three days hence and those who were belated in their preparations began frantically packing belongings in the rawhide packs.

Sun Boy was hardly up on the morning of departure before the first of the big lodges came down. Each family worked to fold and pack the lodge cover on a pole-drag, along with their personal effects. Young men rounded up the loose horses of the band, holding them in a nearby meadow until the procession was under way. The horse herd would bring up the rear, to avoid creating dust in the column itself.

It was on the second afternoon of travel that they encountered the Head Splitters. Cabeza, riding at the front of the column with Heads Off, Long Elk, and Sanchez, reached for his lance.

"No, put it away, Ramon," chuckled Heads Off. "There will be no fighting."

"These are not Head Splitters?"

"Yes, but they have their women and children with them and so do we. Neither group will risk a fight."

The two columns circled warily and soon, in the manner Cabeza had already seen, three men detached themselves from the other party and cantered forward.

"Long Elk, Ramon, come." The chief casually kneed his horse forward.

"*Ah-koh,*" the enemy chief greeted, extending his right hand upward, palm forward. Then he began to signal.

"You have found good hunting?"

"Yes," answered Heads Off, also in hand talk. "Very good. The weather is good."

Cabeza was dumbfounded. He was certain these were men of the same band they had visited and later fought. Yet here they sat, calmly talking about the weather with their mortal enemies.

"The Hairfaces winter with you?"

"No, they go south. Some of us go with them."

An animated conversation had now started between two of the Head Splitters, with one pointing to Cabeza's horse.

"That is the horse of Lean Bull," signed one.

Cabeza shook his head.

"That is the horse of *me*," he gestured. "It was the horse of Lean Bull when he was alive."

There were exclamations of surprise and awe. Obviously, these warriors did not know until now of Lean Bull's demise.

"One of our women killed him," Long Elk shrugged matter-of-factly.

This was the ultimate in insults, a twisting of the thorn in the flesh. Considering the Head Splitters' low esteem of women, there could be no worse way to meet one's death than at the hands of one of the women of the People.

"Lean Bull was crazy anyway," observed the Head Splitter chief.

It seemed a good place to end the conversation and Heads Off calmly reined his horse around. The Head Splitters gripped their weapons, but made no overt move. The emissaries rode slowly back toward their own groups.

"I don't understand, Juan. There is no fighting? You talked to their chief almost like old friends."

"What would you do, Ramon? Neither side can afford to start anything. We will fight another time. Long Elk did overdo the thing about our women a little," he chuckled. "Did you see how furious they were?"

"Do you meet them often like this?"

"Yes, nearly every year. It's a time for swapping threats about what we'll do to each other next time. Nothing ever comes of it."

The two columns circled cautiously and moved on. No more Head Splitters were seen.

With good weather holding and easy traveling, the People reached winter camp in good condition. The temptation to stay was strong for Cabeza, but responsibility prevailed and, after a day's final preparation, the party set off for the long trip to the coast.

For the young Elk-dog men, it was an exciting adventure, a chance to see new country. For the others, each step was nearer home. South Wind, alone, was leaving the land of her home, probably never to return. She was so completely occupied, however, with the joy of her marriage to Cabeza, that Heads Off was certain she would do well. Many men, he knew, took foreign wives back to Spain and South Wind should be able to hold her own anywhere.

The girl turned to wave once more as the group set off.

Travel was rapid, much more so than with the entire band. This was a party composed of horsemen, mobile and well armed. They were able to achieve much better speed, in fact, than on the trip north. Now there was no uncertainty, no question as to their goal. They could push ahead as fast as horses and riders were able to tolerate.

Perhaps one of the more striking differences on this trip was the change in Sanchez. The little man had seemed to grow in stature and in self-esteem. He had become quite a respectable marksman with the crossbow. He had friends now among the lancers. Even his relationship to Lizard was changed. It was amazing to see how the stresses of the expedition, the imminent threat of death, had hardened and tempered the soft personality into a keen and resilient individual.

Much of this was merely noticed by the others and was completely overlooked by Sanchez. In his mind, he only wished to get back to civilization, as represented by an everpresent supply of food and wine and the occasional comfort of a feminine companion. He had completely forgotten that one of his original aims for this expedition was the opportunity to steal from those who had more than Sanchez. And that, of course, was practically everyone.

40

>> >> >>

It was not until many months later that Sanchez actually became objective in his thinking. He was sitting in the dim of a musty cantina, where he had spent many of his waking hours since his return. He was surrounded by friends. He had friends most of the time now, since he had money.

Sanchez was recalling the many things which had happened to him in the past two years. Their trip home had been unremarkable. They had found the garrison on the river without event and suffered a severe verbal reprimand for crossing the river from the officer in charge. When he learned they had no more silver, even that subsided.

The officer cast covetous glances at South Wind, but Cabeza's attitude clearly said that he would tolerate no nonsense. Even had Cabeza not been present, many of the party would cheerfully have given their lives in the defense of the spirited girl. It had not been forgotten that she had been their only warning of treachery by the Head Splitters.

So it happened that Sergeant Perez had been obliged to give some fatherly advice in due course of time. Noticing a lustful leer on the face of the officer as he watched the swing of South Wind's graceful body, the grizzled sergeant had sidled close.

"Lieutenant, she killed a man once for a look no worse than that. If she hadn't, I have at least six men who would have."

The lieutenant was impressed enough by the tone and obvious sincerity that he did not proceed to question the precise accuracy of the remark. However, he kept his thoughts more carefully concealed.

Oliviera had sailed the *Paloma* into the bay at precisely the appointed time. They had bid good-bye to Lizard with some regret. He had become well respected for his contribution. He was also an influential man among his own people now.

A similar melancholy had fallen over the little group when they reached home shores. They had given much, had invested a portion of their lives in each other. It was hard to think that they would never be together again.

The attorney of Don Pedro Garcia had talked to them. The old man had set up an intricate plan to pay bonus money in addition to their regular pay for those who successfully returned. Sanchez, in the event of success in the finding of Juan Garcia, was to receive a handsome stipend, which was now awarded to him. Likewise, Ramon Cabeza was well rewarded.

Then the group had scattered. The Garcia servants, of course, would return to the service of *Doña* Isabel Garcia.

Several of the professional soldiers found jobs waiting for men of such experience in the New World.

Ramon Cabeza had nearly decided that the life of a professional soldier was not to his liking. Now that he was a married man, it seemed hardly a fit existence. Consequently, it was without great regret that he accepted his father's suggestion. The elder Cabeza, failing in health, wished to turn over the reins of his vast ranch holdings to his son. Immediately, Ramon Cabeza hired Sergeant Perez to help manage the horse-breeding portion of the Cabeza interests.

Sanchez, for his part, had been drunk for two weeks. None of the cheap red house wine for this man of means. He ordered only the best and the innkeepers were happy to oblige. To take advantage, even, of the fact that Sanchez really knew very little of any but the poorest of wines.

And he had been surrounded by friends. Never, in all his life, had he had so many. Sanchez bought round after round of wine and the parties lasted until far into the small hours. Sometimes all night.

Just now he was drunk, a little sad, and feeling very sorry for one Sanchez. He sipped his good red wine and only felt worse. A tawdry bar girl tried to sit on his lap and he pushed her gently away. He needed to think.

Why, in Christ's name, why? How could anyone, surrounded by food, wine, and friends, feel unhappy? In a half-drunken stupor, he tried to remember how it had been before he had money. He remembered that he had usually drunk alone. An acquaintance staggered past, arm around the waist of a hard-looking woman. He stopped and, above the din of the crowd in the inn, shouted in Sanchez's ear.

"Hey, *amigo*, we need more wine!"

Automatically, Sanchez reached into the purse at his belt and tossed a couple of gold coins to the innkeeper. The man nodded, pleased, and scurried off to the cellar.

The other customer gave Sanchez a drunken smile and pounded him heartily across the shoulders. Strange, thought Sanchez, I thought it felt good for people to like me. It had, on the prairies of New Spain. He had relished the respect that he had felt from the other members of the party. And he had had no money then.

It was all very puzzling, the more so since he was so very drunk. His fuzzy thoughts refused to congeal and he tried to focus them.

Let's see now, that one had just asked him for more money for wine. What if he had had no more money? Would he have no more friends? He looked around at an unkempt individual sleeping with his head on the next table, his wine spilling into his beard. He couldn't even remember the man's name.

He could remember the names of men who had respected him in New Spain. Cabeza, Perez, Don Pedro, Lizard, yes, even Heads Off, Long Elk, and Standing Bird.

A tear of self-pity ran down the cheek of Sanchez and dropped into his wine. He wished he were with some of those companions, men with whom he had shared and suffered.

Perez had gone to work for Ramon Cabeza. He, Sanchez, had never had employment, had little understanding of what it meant. But Perez could do it. It would mean being with men he had come to admire. Maybe Cabeza would hire him, Sanchez. It would do no harm to ask.

Sanchez stood, a little unsteady on his feet, but standing taller and with more pride than at any time since he was paid and said good-bye to the others. He threaded his way among the tables toward the door. The innkeeper, alarmed at the threat of losing his best paying customer, scurried after him.

"*Señor* Sanchez," he fawned, "we need more money for the wine and the dancers."

Sanchez looked at the man for a long moment, then slowly reached into his leather purse and drew out a handful of gold and silver coins of various denominations. He let them drop slowly through his fingers to bounce on the puncheon floor. The innkeeper scuttled around, trying to pick them up.

Sanchez glanced back at the revelers, dancing, drinking, staggering. One man crouched in a corner, vomiting from overindulgence, and a girl laughed drunkenly. Sanchez turned back to the barkeep.

"When that is gone," he said, pointing to the handful of coins, "throw them out!"

He passed through the doorway and out into the cool night air. He threw back his shoulders and strode purposefully down the street. He would go in the morning to talk to Cabeza. It could do no harm.

About the Author

>> >> >>

DON COLDSMITH was born in Iola, Kansas, in 1926. He served as a World War II combat medic in the South Pacific and returned to his native state where he graduated from Baker University in 1949 and received his M.D. from the University of Kansas in 1958. He worked at several jobs before entering medical school: he was a YMCA group counselor, a gunsmith, a taxidermist, and for a short time, a Congregational preacher. In addition to his private medical practice, Dr. Coldsmith is a staff physician at Emporia State University's Health Center, teaches in the English Department, and is active as a freelance writer, lecturer, and rancher. He and his wife of 26 years, Edna, have raised five daughters.

Dr. Coldsmith produced the first ten novels in "The Spanish Bit Saga" in a five-year period; he writes and revises the stories first in his head, then in longhand. From this manuscript he reads aloud to his wife, whom he calls his "chief editor." Finally the finished version is skillfully typed by his longtime office receptionist.

Of his decision to create, or re-create, the world of the Plains Indian in the 16th and 17th centuries, the author says: "There has been very little written about this time period. I wanted also to portray these Native Americans as human beings, rather than as stereotyped 'Indians.' That word does not appear anywhere in the series—for a reason. As I have researched the time and place, the indigenous cultures, it's been a truly inspiring experience for me."